Clifton Bridge

Stories of Innocence and Experience from Pakistan

IRSHAD ABDULKADIR

HarperCollins *Publishers* India

First published in 2013 by
HarperCollins *Publishers* India

Copyright © Irshad AbdulKadir 2013

ISBN: 978-93-5029-618-9

2 4 6 8 10 9 7 5 3 1

HarperCollins Publishers
A-53, Sector 57, Noida, Uttar Pradesh 201301, India
77-85 Fulham Palace Road, London W6 8JB, United Kingdom
Hazelton Lanes, 55 Avenue Road, Suite 2900, Toronto, Ontario M5R 3L2
and 1995 Markham Road, Scarborough, Ontario M1B 5M8, Canada
25 Ryde Road, Pymble, Sydney, NSW 2073, Australia
31 View Road, Glenfield, Auckland 10, New Zealand
10 East 53rd Street, New York NY 10022, USA

Typeset in 11/15 Charter BT
by Jojy Philip, New Delhi 110 015

Printed and bound at
Thomson Press (India) Ltd.

Clifton Bridge

Stories of Innocence and Experience from Pakistan

Irshad AbdulKadir is a graduate of Cambridge University and a Barrister at Law. He is also a lecturer in legal studies specializing in common law traditions and reasoning. Several articles written by him on socio-economics, governance and politics have appeared in newspapers and journals. He is noted too as a theatre critic and a civil rights activist. This is his first work of fiction.

For Iman, Aliya and Dayyan …
and of course, Reggie.

Contents

All in the Family

Razia and Daud were cousins and, as was customary in their community, their marriage had been decided upon almost since birth. Razia had been brought up to regard Daud as the most important person in her life. It was not quite the same for him. He was more casual about the association. His approach towards her was pragmatic, occasionally distant, but always correct. The difference in their commitment to the marriage dismayed Razia, but she remained the loyal wife.

She was more than simply that. She took an interest in his work too. Daud had a share in a family fabric franchise. He had limited ambition, confident of a livelihood always being there. She felt that he had sold himself short.

By gleaning information from elders experienced in the cloth trade, Razia acquired enough knowledge to steer Daud away from the tightly controlled domestic operation towards a modest but independent store in a major retail centre. A few years later, egged on by Razia, he was running a cotton-ginning factory and exporting yarn.

Razia also gave him a family – three sons and a daughter – and an identity. She persuaded Daud to leave the joint family 'arrangement' in Saddar for a flat in an old part of town, which she grandly dubbed 'Daud Manzil'. She even wangled an honorary post for him in the cloth merchants' business council.

Success had, however, come at a price. Relations between them had ebbed over the years. Razia even looked the other way when there were seaside frolics with business cronies and call girls – on Fridays after congregational prayers when uprightness gave way to licence. At times, she had to contend with embarrassment over financial indiscretions and bungled deals. Despite his shortcomings, she found herself guiding him towards the right move, the correct gesture. But the effort took its toll. Years of buttressing Daud turned Razia's wholesomeness into a tight-lipped gauntness dominated by dark-ringed eyes.

※

Malika sat by the windowsill in her bedroom looking down at the paved courtyard. People had been calling to condole the death of her father. She dreaded the future. To be stuck in a village forty-seven miles from Multan was bad enough, but to be twenty-eight without any prospect of marriage was worse. And now – with her father, Chaudhry Amanatullah Khan, gone – it was more than she could bear.

She had been a sort of social outcast since the local Makhdoom's son had, without explanation, broken off his engagement with her. It was rumoured that he did so on discovering – during the exuberance of a physical encounter – that she was not a virgin.

Unlike her brothers and mother, her father was understanding and sympathetic to her. Without him, she would have to face their contempt alone. She longed to be in a place far from the village, from the family, anywhere – Karachi, Lahore, Islamabad, even Quetta would do. While feeling inordinately sorry for herself, she was distracted momentarily by some of the visitors. One of them stood out. Unlike the locals, he was dressed in a shirt and trousers, and carried a bag. Only when her brothers addressed him as 'Uncle Daud' – all hugging and breaking down – did she know who he was.

❈

Malika had long been curious about her father's 'dearer than life' friend. She recalled Amanat going on about him endlessly. Daud and Amanat had been inseparable, when young, despite belonging to different communities. Daud was a Gujrati-speaking Bohra from Karachi. Amanat belonged to Multan and spoke Seraiki. The bond between them had cut across the distance. They parted tearfully when Amanat had to return to Multan to take charge of ancestral land.

And now, Daud had come to Multan from Karachi to mourn the loss of his friend.

❧

The guests departed after the evening meal, leaving a handful of friends and relatives squatting on carpeted floors. Fresh food was laid out. Daud's wandering eye spied the curvaceous presence of Malika in the circle of veiled women seated around the *dastarkhan*.

Later, while sipping green tea he commiserated with Amanat's widow, offering help, services and sympathy.

'He was more than a brother,' he murmured.

'Well then, as the wife of your brother ... I want you to find a husband for your niece Malika.'

Daud was taken aback at the request. Malika squirmed and looked away.

That night, after knocking gently on Daud's door, Malika slipped into the room in the guise of a maidservant. To his surprise, she sat on the floor beside his bed and proceeded to massage his legs, telling him that the mistress had instructed her to do so. His resistance was brushed aside by persuasive hands.

She returned the following night. On the third night – by which time he had discovered her true identity – Daud drew her into bed.

❧

For a while Razia could not breathe. Blood drained away making her dizzy. The room seemed to whirl around. She stumbled. Her son, Altaf, dropped the telefax, reaching out to support her. The message from Multan said it all: *Daud Sahib sends salams. He got married this morning to Chaudhry Amanat's daughter, Malika. Everything will be explained when he gets back…*

On returning to Karachi, Daud lodged Malika in Arambagh in a colonial sandstone house which he shared with grain merchants, who used their portion of the place for storage. The rest was taken over by Malika.

Razia waited for three days before she finally heard his footsteps. Her loss of face within the community was nothing compared to the loss of faith in Daud. He justified the marriage as fulfilment of an obligation to Amanat. She suspected there was more to it than just that. '*You* are my family,' he said reassuringly.

'You have more than one family now.'

'What would you've done in my place?'

'I don't know … *but I do know* … I'd never have let you down … as you've done again and again…'

'Razia … Razia … control yourself.'

'Yes … that's what I'm always expected to do … so be it … Will you have some tea?'

He stayed for a week at Daud Manzil, then moved to Arambagh, returning a week later. He made full use of the choice of alternative homes. Razia resumed the role of attentive wife somewhat mechanically. In her private moments, she cursed Malika and prayed for her undoing.

Malika's expectations of a cushy life as the wife of a thriving mill owner were dashed when she saw the crumbling masonry. Daud made no bones about being tight-fisted.

She was also tiring of his middle-aged embraces. She wanted a flat of her own – like Razia's. To make her point, she drew Daud's attention to the peeling plaster and snake tracks in the compound indicating the presence of reptiles in the Arambagh granaries. Daud made vague promises and turned away.

※

Six months later, news of Malika's pregnancy filled Razia with horror. She resorted to black magic, invoking spells learnt from faqirs to ward off the event.

Twice a week, she would retire to the kitchen at

midnight to make a potion and perform other rituals. She prepared the potion by mixing measured portions of castor oil, linseed, bitter gourd juice and neem leaves in an earthenware pot placed on a coal fire. As it started to simmer, she added onion peel, chicken heads, fish bones, shrimp shells and bitter almonds, all the while chanting imprecations ending with the refrain: 'Out black spot … begone!'

When the mixture boiled over, she strained it through a sieve, letting the putrid broth cool before pouring it into vials. Then she undid her chignon and sashayed around the kitchen swinging her head, thrashing her hair and intoning curses punctuated by the refrain. By the time the dance reached a crescendo, she was almost shrieking, 'Out black spot … cursed spot … hellish spot … begone … vanish.'

The contents of the vials, representing the head, heart and innards were emptied daily, drop by drop in a bed of live coals, at sunrise, noon and sunset, accompanied by more frenzied incantations.

It was destined: Malika's baby was stillborn. Further pregnancies ended the same way. Razia believed the witchcraft was working. And who was to say it was not? Razia relished the idea of being the mother of the only children Daud had.

✽

Malika tried to offset Daud's disappointment over her failure to provide him with children by appealing to his promiscuous nature. Arambagh now became the scene of bizarre orgies orchestrated by Malika, in which call girls from Napier Road played a major part.

Rumours soon reached Razia of the havoc Malika was playing with her husband. This provided her with the fuel she needed to score points against Malika in the community. Malika, being wary of Razia, kept her distance, calling her a 'dried old witch'. Daud knew that there was no love lost between the women, but managed to avoid taking sides. The feud worked to his advantage as both women fought to hold his interest.

While Razia kept busy with domestic chores and parenting her family, Malika had little to do when Daud was away. So she spent time browsing through glossy film magazines, gossiping on the cellphone and watching DVD recordings of Bollywood movies, until she spotted the Pathan supervisor of the granary.

To avoid her maid's curious eye, she enticed him to a cellar under the living room, where they made love on an improvised bed of basmati rice. After that they kept in touch, meeting whenever possible: on the roof, at the granary counter, in the cellar and sometimes on a grassy patch at the back of the house – unaware of the maid watching.

❈

Daud was persuaded by business colleagues to diversify his business interests by investing in a beauty salon planned for a bustling shopping mall. Razia disapproved of the scheme. Despite her objections, Daud joined the venture as working partner.

Daud busied himself interviewing prospective employees, while an interior designer flitted about supervising the decoration and furnishing of the new premises. When it came to appointing a hair stylist, a pretty young thing called Shireen was selected – because Daud was drawn to her. In the normal course of events, the attraction would have subsided after he had had his fill of her, but it took a different turn because he became besotted.

There were other complications. Shireen was a Parsi and she was virtuous. She rebuffed Daud's overtures and left the job. Daud was distraught. He had never experienced such feelings for a woman before. He felt he had to have her at all costs. So he pursued her relentlessly. She was unmoved, threatening to file a complaint of harassment.

Daud's lack of interest in the business was becoming apparent to the staff. Even his son, Altaf, felt something was amiss. He was especially alarmed by the fruit baskets sent to a Ms Shireen Dubash at Parsi Colony.

Altaf wasted no time in reporting these developments to his mother. Razia's concern at Daud marrying Malika was nothing compared to the panic that swept over her when told of Shireen. She gauged the enormity of the problem when she saw Daud crestfallen and quite broken by Shireen's rejection.

Daud was at his worst when the inconceivable happened. Shireen discovered that she was interested after all, but she wanted nothing less than marriage. The news was received with relief by Daud's friends but came as a thunderbolt to Razia.

Collecting her wits, Razia tried to focus on ways and means to checkmate another wedding. Daud's second marriage was a fait accompli about which she could do nothing. This time she was determined to act pre-emptively.

I've been betrayed once, she mused, *not again … never again … even if I've to fight Daud … for the sake of the children.*

She saw Shireen as a potential threat to her family interests. While she was convinced that her spells had prevented Malika from having live babies, she was uncertain whether they would be effective the second time round. She felt the need to muster all resources to pull off a successful coup d'état. The only ally that came to mind was Malika.

So she boarded a rickshaw and set off for Arambagh

for the first time in her life, to call on someone whose face she had sworn never to see.

Malika was nervous at the prospect of Razia's visit. She guessed that the impending marriage had prompted the move but was unable to see how their meeting could make any difference to the outcome.

The awkwardness of the encounter was somewhat dispelled by the gifts Razia produced while the maid assisted her in removing her abaya.

Malika and Razia sized each other up over tea, both amazed at the close resemblance of the actual person to the imagined version.

'Malika Behen,' Razia said at last, 'you know ... we're both threatened by this Shireen creature.'

'Apart from having to share our husband with her, how're we threatened ... Baji?'

'If she has children, they'll have rights in family property.'

'That concerns those who have children ... as for me ... unless I have children who survive ... I can only claim a widow's share ... who can deny me that?'

Razia paused before speaking, 'You stand to lose everything ... if he divorces you.'

'Why would he divorce me?' Malika asked in astonishment.

A sound from the interior of the house made them look up. The maid, busy eavesdropping, stepped back into the kitchen to avoid being seen. The interruption helped Razia choose words that would have the effect she wanted.

'For betraying him.'

'What do you mean?' gasped Malika, jumping up from her chair, visibly shaken.

Having made her point, Razia became conciliatory. 'I'm not blaming you for anything ... but *he* will ... if he comes to know ... what's been going on here ... with the Pathan.'

Trapped, Malika sank back in the chair and asked meekly, 'What do you want from me?'

'Do as I say ... I'm trying to prevent the marriage ... if you help, I'll see you get your rights.'

There was a pause. Malika did a rapid mental review of options that would secure her interests before deciding to go with Razia.

'There is a way,' she said, eyes narrowing suggestively.

'If it works,' Razia said, 'I promise you a larger share than you are due ... even if I've to give you part of my portion ... do you have something in mind?'

'Yes, I do. It'll give you and me complete control of his property.'

'What're you getting at?'

'Just that. If my plan succeeds, I want one-third of the property.'

'One-third? That's too much.'

'Promise me that, and I'll give you a workable scheme.'

Razia wavered, then held out her hand. 'I promise – one-third to you if it works ... now tell me.'

'I want some guarantee first that you'll keep your word.'

Razia pondered a while, then took off her gem-studded gold bracelets, nose stud and diamond tops and handed them to Malika.

'Here, keep these as a token of my promise.'

Malika got up and bolted a door to the inner rooms. Hearing the door shut, the maid sidled out of the kitchen and placed her ear against the door panels, but could not hear a thing.

❊

A few days later Malika called Daud and congratulated him. He was surprised.

'You're not upset ... like Razia?'

'What for? I'm also an additional wife.'

'Will you attend the wedding then?'

'Of course. I'll even help in the selection of Shireen's outfit ... if you like.'

'That's great, Malika, jani.'

'I'll pick out some bridal wear from designer boutiques on approval. You can stop by tomorrow evening ... see what you like.'

'That's wonderful ... truly wonderful.'

The next day Malika arranged for a selection of glittering garments to be displayed in the living room. She also ordered dinner for three. Altaf dropped in during the afternoon with a largish jewellery chest which he said his mother had sent. Malika had the chest placed in the cellar for safe keeping.

Daud came after dark, brimming with expectation. He was dazzled by the finery. While going over it, Malika said, 'I have a surprise for you.'

'What kind of surprise?'

Just then the doorbell rang.

'You'll see in a moment,' she replied.

The maid came in looking stunned, gesticulating wildly. She was followed by Razia. It was Daud's turn to look stunned.

During dinner Daud was overcome with affection for both his wives. He felt blessed that all grievances were forgotten – his family had come together at last.

After dinner Razia enquired about the chest.

'What chest?' Daud asked

'The one Razia Baji sent,' Malika explained, 'with some of your mother's jewellery ... for the new bride.'

'You did that?' Daud exclaimed in amazement to Razia.

'Well, she'll be her daughter-in-law too, won't she?' Razia remarked, beaming.

'Where is it?' Daud asked, beside himself.

'I put it away in the cellar,' Malika said. 'Perhaps you should go down and get it.'

'But it's heavy, and it must be dark down there,' Razia said.

'Yes,' Malika confirmed, 'the bulb's fused … take my torch.'

'Don't try to haul it up the steps … just bring individual boxes,' Razia said. 'Here, take the key.'

Daud eagerly lifted a trapdoor in the floor of the living room and descended, torch and key in hand. As the trapdoor closed, Razia moved and stood upon it while Malika swiftly bolted the door leading to the kitchen. Both froze on hearing muffled sounds from the cellar.

After what seemed ages, there was a strangulated sound, followed by screams. The women were rooted, staring fixedly at each other. They could hear laboured breathing, sounds of clambering footsteps and Daud's voice pleading to be let out. Suddenly the trapdoor was pushed from below by a desperate heave. The movement dislodged Razia. Both women leapt on the trapdoor in a flash and held each other in place. They remained motionless, listening to the frantic scratching and banging under their feet mingled with piteous cries of 'Razia', 'Malika'.

After a while the pounding abated. The sounds became faint and then subsided. Some weighty object seemed to slither down the steps to the cellar floor. Then deafening silence.

The police report described the cause of death as 'multiple snake bites'. There were several snake tracks on the scattered basmati rice, a lit torch lay next to the body and nothing else.

Clifton Bridge

On the day Peeru discovered the mosque near Clifton Bridge, he was caught trying to steal a ride on a bus. He had got away in the past by claiming he was a minor. Not on this occasion though. The bus conductor was unmoved and made him pay full fare. Peeru did not know his age, or the circumstances of his birth. By counting on his fingers, he worked out that he was somewhere between seventeen and nineteen.

Peeru's earliest memories were of an unsettled existence in Karachi with cross-eyed Jumma during which he slept in the open, was beaten, made to beg, and was always hungry. Their first 'home' – a lean-to against the boundary wall of a cement factory – came about when Rano joined the ragged duo. Peeru always remembered the first meal – boiled rice and lentils –

prepared by her. She told him to call her 'Amma' and later enrolled him in classes at the factory mosque.

Peeru and Jumma had come across Rano wandering dazedly around Karachi City station – with a black eye and minus two teeth. Jumma offered her bed, board and male protection in what he called 'a ravenous city'. In time, Rano disclosed that she had been condemned as a *siyah kari* – or evil woman – by her peasant community in Sind owing to her becoming pregnant several months after her husband had died. A kindly policeman had saved her from being stoned to death by putting her on a Karachi-bound train.

When the midwife placed a swaddled Noori beside Rano, Peeru felt part of a family for the first time, even though he did not look upon Jumma as his father.

Within days of Noori's birth, the lean-to structures were bulldozed by civic authorities. Jumma moved with his ragtag band to a burgeoning slum in the Lyari riverbed. The new home was pervaded by the stench of sewerage, being a step away from the channel that bore city effluent to the sea. It was during the Lyari years that two additional babies, Billa and Zeebu, joined them.

Billa was fair-skinned and blue-eyed. He had been lifted from a hospital crib and given to Jumma as payment in kind for facilitating a burglary. Skinny little Zeebu arrived a few years later. She belonged to the same tribe as Rano, and had been placed in Rano's arms by her mother who had died in prison.

※

As he grew older, Peeru was upgraded by Jumma from beggary to street crimes. He learnt how to pick pockets, rifle push carts, shoplift and burgle.

'If you want to become a smart street operator, master these skills,' directed Jumma.

What if I don't?

'What?'

'I said, yes … yes … of course … I will.'

But when he tried to skip practising with knife, cudgel and gun, by pleading a toothache, Jumma struck him across the face, felling him.

'Bastard, stop pretending, you'll end up with your stomach ripped open unless you learn to defend yourself.'

'Baba, I really can't do any more now,' Peeru protested, wiping a bleeding nose with the back of his hand. 'We can try later.'

'Get up, motherfucker, or I'll cut you up and throw your carcass in the gutter along with dead cats, dogs and other floating shit…'

With the youngsters, Jumma was a whip-wielding ringmaster. He perfected them in sharp practices according to age. Noori, as a baby, was borne on hip by Rano on begging forays because a starving child always evoked sympathy. At four, she was replaced at Rano's side by Billa and planted at traffic stopovers with a begging bowl. A few years later, little Zeebu took over from Billa, who learnt to wipe windscreens and sell bric-a-brac to car-borne commuters. Whenever hungry, they scrounged food and took home extras.

The daily routine lasted from 10 a.m. till 7 p.m. At day's end, Jumma collected the takings. Anyone failing to bring the amount set by him was beaten. The children slept on the floor oblivious to heat, cold, stench and vermin. There was no electricity or water. A solitary cot was reserved for Jumma. When he felt the need for company, Rano joined him.

During a freak rainstorm, the Lyari shack was swept away by a sudden flooding of the riverbed. Salvaging possessions from the putrid sludge, the hapless clan squatted in the lower segment of the spandrel under Clifton Bridge, a humpback colonial landmark in an affluent residential area with trees and wide roads. It was like heaven after Lyari.

Jumma soon set up operations in the new neighbourhood, assigning each child to a specific spot. Rano, infant in her arms, moved from one to another, begging and keeping watch. Peeru dropped them off at their beats and collected them on his way home. In between, he was at Jumma's beck and call for petty crimes – swiping untended cellphones, carrier bags, goods in shopping malls and the occasional wallet.

To escape from Jumma, Peeru started to go to the neigbourhood Baitus Salah mosque where he befriended a boy who swept and mopped floors. The muezzin's call had intrigued him since his first lessons. He found the right to enter the premises without being checked novel and strangely empowering.

'It's a good place, Amma,' he told Rano, 'because I'm equal to everyone else there.'

He came to know the prayer ritual by following the members of the congregation.

'I stood between a judge and a butcher for the Friday prayer,' he boasted to Rano.

The tranquillity of breezy cloisters punctuated by the muted patter of barefoot worshippers on tiled floors was soothing. There were moments when he felt strangely elated. He did not know why. It was something very special.

'What do you do there?' Rano asked.

'There's so much going on … flowers and leaves are painted along the walls of the prayer hall … and Quranic letters everywhere which seem to move if you look at them long enough … Allah's names written in coin-shaped tablets painted on the interior of the dome … there are traces of incense … The minarets are like arms reaching upward to Allah…'

'How have you come to know such things?'

'I've learnt from the boy who tends the mosque from reciting the namaz to cleansing myself for prayer. Would you believe it there's no shortage of water there, unlike everywhere else in the city including Clifton Road. I even share meals with students and instructors.'

'Meals?' Rano queried.

'Yes, people send all kinds of food … biryani and halwa … fruit and sherbet.'

'It seems like … like … heaven,' she said, looking at his shining eyes.

'It's … it's so peaceful … not like the dirty, noisy world outside.'

'You've a gentle soul to match your gentle face,' Rano said, drawing his head to her shoulder. 'Wonder what'll become of you.'

❀

While Peeru ogled at female forms displayed on billboards at traffic intersections, Noori looked upon them as role models. There was an earthiness about her – a dusky, dark-haired childwoman ripening early in the season. She painted her face with stolen cosmetics and swayed her hips when on her beat.

'You'll get into trouble,' Peeru cautioned her, 'looking like that.'

Jumma also noticed the change. He would have

assaulted her one night if Rano had not held up a meat chopper and Peeru not doused him with a bucketful of water. The next day Rano told Peeru that Noori's continued presence in the shack was risky. She suggested marriage as a way out, tasking him with finding a suitable mate.

Jumma scoffed at the idea. 'Who'll marry her except another beggar,' he sneered. 'Trash will only beget trash.' He wanted to sell her to a high bidder or set her up in a brothel.

Noori surprised all of them by bolting with a fast-talking adman who offered a modelling contract and promised to get her into films.

'You'll see me soon on a marquee,' she called out to Peeru as she was whisked away by a taxi, amid expensive cars, over Clifton Bridge.

Peeru waved back, pleased at her decision. He felt it was a better option than marriage or prostitution.

Of course, she's taking a chance, he thought, *but at least she'll get to do what she wants.*

Rano was inconsolable at the loss of her daughter.

'The only child of my body … gone,' she wailed, beating her breast.

'What child,' Jumma sneered, 'that ungrateful bastard, who almost brought about your death by stoning?'

He was livid at being deprived of the chance of making a windfall profit on account of Noori's elopement. Even a successful carjacking in which Peeru risked his life failed to stem his black mood.

Peeru could sense a change in Jumma. He saw him conversing at street corners with strangers, or planning furtively on the cellphone. One afternoon, he came laden with sweets and chocolates which he gave to Billa and Zeebu. He explained they were donations from a charitable organization run by some kind ladies. The following day, he brought a fruit basket and later a colourful assortment of clothes for them.

'When I go again, I'll take you with me,' he promised Billa and Zeebu, 'so that you can thank them.'

Peeru instinctively felt there was more to the matter.

When Peeru spotted Jumma and Billa perched precariously on the footboard of an overcrowded bus, he followed. At the Saddar terminus, they boarded a rickshaw. Peeru gave chase in another rickshaw. The route led through bazaars to a run-down house with a simulated Victorian façade off Bhurgari Road.

Peeru, concealed by a bougainvillea bush, saw Jumma take Billa into the house. After what seemed ages, Jumma came out alone, hopped on to his rickshaw and sped away. Panicking, Peeru ventured towards the house, but was ordered off by a guard who appeared suddenly. So he waited, unsure what else to do.

In the late afternoon, some armed men came out of the house carrying a blanketed bundle. They boarded a four-wheel drive. As it drove off, a gust lifted a tarpaulin flap, revealing Billa pinioned in the rear compartment, his mouth wide open in a silent scream. Peeru ran after the vehicle for as long as it was in sight, calling out to Billa, begging the men to stop, cursing them.

Distraught, he sought police help. They advised him to forget the incident as the odds were against him. Billa was a stolen child *not* related to him. His purchaser, an influential feudal with a penchant for slave boys, had successfully evaded such charges in the past.

On coming home, Peeru saw the new motorcycle, shotgun and flashy clothes Jumma had bought.

'Blood money,' he choked.

Jumma got up to hit him, but soon thought better of it. After all, Peeru had grown taller than him and his clenched fists and red-rimmed eyes made him look menacing.

'He belonged to me, I dealt with him as I chose,' Jumma was defiant. 'Besides, Billa will be much better off now.'

'He belonged to all of us.' Rano began to cry.

'Nothing belongs to you, not even your lives. Without me, you'll perish,' Jumma raged.

'Allah gave us life,' Peeru said quietly.

Ignoring his remark, Jumma revved up the motorcycle and offered to take Zeebu for a ride.

'Never,' Peeru muttered.

Things were wrong – very wrong. Peeru realized

that something had to be done to stop Jumma from destroying their lives but decision-making did not come readily to him. He was accustomed to following orders. He went to the mosque, hoping to find his friend and was told that he had gone away to join the mujahidin.

At a loss, he paced the premises after the last congregation had dispersed. He lay down finally in the courtyard. He gazed at the starlit sky and realized he was all alone. He was woken up some time later by the imam.

'Why are you here at this hour?'

Peeru blinked at the enquiring bearded face not knowing what to say.

'You seem troubled ... can I help?'

The first words of concern he heard that day brought tears to his eyes. Sobbing, he clutched the imam's ankles.

In the lighted interior of an antechamber, Peeru nibbled naan dipped in sugary tea.

'I've seen you before slipping in and out of the mosque, like a shadow,' the imam said, 'and wondered about you ... why such distress?'

Peeru told him as much as he could recall, then asked the imam if he should go to the police.

'That won't help. Nothing illegal is happening at present. There are only your fears. Besides, an operator like Jumma must have connections in the police.'

'What shall I do then?'

'Pray for guidance.'

'Don't know how.'

The imam looked at him intently, hesitating a while.

'I'll refer to certain passages in the Quran which may help with your problem,' he said finally. 'When their meaning is clear, it's up to you to do what you regard right. Also remember that our doors are always open...'

Peeru watched fascinated as the imam raised his hands, invoking God's help in resolving the dilemma. Afterwards he meditated, consulted books, clicked on his desktop PC and made notes before turning to Peeru.

'The suras I'll cite deal with fighting against evil symbolized by Satan, justifiable killing of vermin and preservation of life.'

Peeru edged closer to focus on his words. The imam quoted from *Sura Al-Nissa, Sura Al-Furqan* and *Sura Al-Maida* in the Quran.

By the time Peeru returned home, Rano was curled up in a corner with her arms around Zeebu. Jumma's cot was empty and the motorcycle was not to be seen. He dropped down exhausted and fell asleep instantly, lulled by the rumblings of late-night traffic over Clifton Bridge.

He was aroused by Zeebu's screams, Rano's protests and Jumma's ranting. Jumma was trying to snatch Zeebu from Rano's arms. From the raised voices, Peeru could make out that Jumma had negotiated the sale of one of Zeebu's kidneys to an organ transplant mafia.

'She has a rare blood group matching a wealthy person's only child ... we'll become rich ... live in a proper house...' Jumma babbled. 'Give her to me...'

'What'll become of Zeebu?' Rano asked.

'She'll be fine with one healthy kidney.'

'You're a liar ... a cheat ... don't trust you.'

'Two-bit village whore ... condemned *siyah kari* ... should've let you rot at the city station instead of sheltering you...'

The struggle continued. Peeru moved in to protect Zeebu. Jumma raised the shotgun, ordering him to release her. Peeru stared at the barrel transfixed. Then the imam's words came flooding back – 'friends of Satan', 'vermin' – and in a flash he saw Jumma as the embodiment of all that. Rano leapt into the fray instinctively to remove Zeebu from the line of fire. She snatched her from Peeru's arms and made for the door. The diversion was long enough for Peeru to wrest the gun from Jumma. Driven by notions of self-defence, saving lives and destroying vermin, he took aim and did what had to be done.

Afterwards there was the sound of rumbling traffic overhead.

'What'll we do now?' Rano asked.

'Seek refuge in the mosque.'

Diva

Sultana was a dreamer. In moments of solitude she drifted into imaginary situations in which she figured somehow. Wafting in air amidst a cluster of butterflies, Sultana would metamorphose into a multicoloured dancer performing before a swaying assembly of foliage, flowers and garden fauna. A ride on a rocking horse transformed into a journey astride the legendary Huma bird winging its way to fabled destinations; or turned into the chariot of a warrior queen battling to save her kingdom. A search for the truth found Sultana on a magic carpet flying between Mohenjodaro and Harappa, unearthing clay tablets with mysterious markings disclosing the Earth's origin.

Such visionary experiences filled her early years. With the passage of time, growing pains created a different awareness – of real changes, mental and physical.

At the age of seventeen, she decided to leave school. Repeated attempts to cajole her back to school failed.

'I've learnt all they can teach,' she explained to her despairing parents.

'How so?' her father quizzed, 'you have no recognized academic qualification, no degree.'

'What good is a degree? I've got my own way of learning,' Sultana insisted.

Her obduracy was something to be reckoned with.

'It's ingrained since birth, wonder where it came from...' her mother grumbled.

'We'll never know,' her father said, walking away.

✻

Sultana learnt to meditate, practised yoga, listened to music and read avidly. Bookshops and libraries were her favourite haunts.

'Look, she didn't want to study and now she's gone and become a bookworm,' her mother remarked with a mix of perplexity and awe.

It was true. Books, mostly on esoteric subjects, mysticism, asceticism, and also books of allegorical verse were to be found everywhere – beneath her pillow, under the bed, in the drawing room, hall or even kitchen.

Sultana also began to attend musical evenings, especially qawwalis, and would occasionally go to poetry recitals.

gangly frame with the floppy hair and dark-rimmed glasses. Suddenly uneasy, she slid out of the room.

❦

'Sultana,' her mother said after the visitors had gone, 'your reactions are so ... so unpredictable. Why did you leave?'

After a pause, Sultana said, 'You saw what happened. I left because it was impossible to remain there.'

'Why?'

'Why? Because *he* was there.'

'Who was there?'

'That ... that ... that young man.'

'The only young man there was Khalid.'

'If that's his name.'

'Sulti, what've you got to do with Khalid?'

'Nothing so far ... nothing...'

'Where did you meet him?'

'I've not met him ... just seen him from time to time. He knows nothing about me.'

A thought struck the mother. 'Do you like him?' she asked.

Regaining her composure, Sultana preferred to leave the question unanswered.

Later, Sultana wondered whether she would see Khalid again. After a week he called on Sultana. When they met – for the first time – it was as if they had known each other for ages. He recalled the collision in the bookshop and admitted to having thought of her.

'You two seemed natural together,' her mother remarked later. 'I've never seen you so happy.'

'God bless and keep you both happy,' the judge said, clearly relieved.

❧

Sultana settled down to married life, content to have Khalid by her side. He was a thoughtful husband. He understood that she needed more space than other women and made sure she got it.

Sultana showed her appreciation by fitting into his social life. She learnt how to entertain with style. And – though she did not relish the thought – she acquired the art of making small talk with bureaucrats, generals, politicians, business magnates and, in short, those who mattered.

At times she would tire of all this and tell Khalid so: 'The pretentiousness, the drunkenness, the illiterate babble of ministers…'

'Sulti, my position at the State Bank demands attendance at these functions. You don't have to come.'

'What a price to pay for a high post. It's unreal … hypocritical.'

Matters came to a head when a minister propositioned

Sultana for 'the favour of one night in exchange for a hefty boost in Khalid's job at the State Bank'.

Affronted, Sultana suggested he advance his own wife's cause with strangers.

'My wife's at home … she avoids mixed gatherings,' he said smugly.

Sultana went home alone that night.

❦

She decided she could take no more. The magic of married life also seemed to be waning. She felt Khalid had changed. The natural grace had hardened into a stiff social posture. His career had taken an upturn and he seemed to have acquired a slight professional edge.

A few weeks later, a medical examination revealed that she was pregnant. Khalid whooped – like a child – when he heard. Amused and already carrying a secret glow, she felt some of the earlier affection return.

In due course, she gave birth to a boy. But her elation on becoming a mother was short-lived, owing partly to postnatal problems. The feeling of fulfilment gave way to a sense of emptiness.

On one occasion, her mother came upon her, with the baby asleep – satiated – in her arms, the tiny mouth disengaged from her breast while Sultana gazed into the distance. 'Strange,' her mother muttered, shaking her head.

Khalid noticed that Sultana was restive. It struck him that she might be bored. So he arranged a 'special' evening for her, asking writers and poets over. Sultana fell in with the idea – circumspectly.

Used to keeping strange hours, the guests came late. They hobbled in unaware as to what was in store. Many knew each other from before. Most of them avoided such gatherings, but had been unable to decline Khalid's invitation partly owing to regard for his father, Dr Abraj Hassan.

Khalid's efforts at striking the right chord that evening failed. Conversation proved limited or stilted. The guests did not mingle, preferring small huddles. Their worst fears came true when they were confronted at twilight with tea – which also meant cakes, samosas and sandwiches.

As a banker, Khalid could scarcely have known that these were bohemians who hankered after other refreshments: bootlegger brands accompanied by specialties such as nan-kebab, tika and haleem.

Sultana realized something was amiss. She had to suppress a giggle when the legendary Sheyba Al Shibli waved an empty hip flask before Khalid, claiming he needed an 'elixir' to keep the poetic juices flowing. Khalid blushed and turned away.

By night, the garden was empty, the high tea untouched. When the last guest had gone Sultana consoled a downcast Khalid.

'Even, if they don't, I appreciate what you did.'

'Don't Sulti ... don't rub it in. It was a mistake, which I won't make again.'

'No, it wasn't ... we'll do it again ... and we'll get it right this time.'

'Why ... how ... what do you have in mind?'

'I want to meet those people I want to meet them on their terms. So we'll have to stock some liquor.'

'Sulti, you know the official line.'

'Don't be so stuffy, Khalid, we've served liquor in the past.'

'Only at private functions, attended by foreign VIPs.'

'Says a lot about hypocrisy.'

So another evening was arranged more in keeping with 'artistic' taste. This time round, Sultana found her way amongst the guests almost by instinct. They also seemed taken by her, recognizing her as a 'kindred spirit'. She was equally at ease with poets and artists. Khalid could not help noticing how relaxed she looked in their company. He could also sense a curious empathy there. It was apparent to him that the idea of 'special' evenings had worked.

One evening when the guests had been lulled into a semi-torpor by a surfeit of poetry, a woman's voice, rich and clear, rang out:

Putting thoughts to word – never so hard as now,

The radiance of your face – never so bright as now.
I dwell in silence, dousing moonbeams with tears,
Razing dreams to stardust, hopes to fears.

It was Sultana, singing a ghazal. When she stopped, there was a hush, followed by a burst of applause. Everyone, including Sultana, was mystified. The sheer purity of the voice had taken them all by surprise. Even she did not know quite how this feat had come about. It had certainly not been altogether voluntary.

'I don't understand what happened,' she said later to Khalid.

❀

On their wedding anniversary, Khalid came home with a diamond bracelet for Sultana. He found her sitting on the carpeted floor in an alcove, eyes closed, strumming a tanpura. She was singing: doing the scales, soaring and dipping with a fluidity that sounded otherworldly. Aware somebody was there, she stopped.

'I didn't know you were so skilled,' Khalid remarked.

'Many things about me, you don't know,' she murmured.

'How is it,' he enquired, 'that you never sang all these years?'

'I did … not long ago … it's as if … something inside has found expression.'

He was taken aback by the edginess in her tone. There was a sense of urgency – desperation perhaps.

'I've decided to take up singing professionally,' she said after a pause.

'Why Sulti?' asked Khalid, puzzled.

'Well, I've been growing within. I seem to have developed a vocal range of eight-and-a-half octaves which is considered exceptional … and more than enough, for traditional music.'

'You mean songs, ghazals and whatever else?'

'Not just that but raags, thumris. In fact, the entire classical repertoire.'

'But why do you need to become professional?'

'Because I'm more than just a 'gifted' amateur to be confined to performing privately.'

'Professionalism has other connotations.'

'True artists are always professional. God has given me something special which I intend to share. That'll only be possible … professionally.'

'But how can you be sure you're actually good enough?'

'Ustaad Maratab Ali of the Gawaliar gharana – the leading exponent of the raag technique – wants to train me. He wouldn't do so if I weren't.'

Khalid felt defeated – and deflated – for the first time in his relationship with Sultana.

It had taken years of tact to manage a capricious

wife and a demanding career. Success in his calling as banker – taking him up to the post of deputy governor of the State Bank – had not come easily. Sultana's interest in professional singing at this juncture came as a complete surprise. He could not see how her new demands would dovetail with his job. Yet he sensed that the note of inevitability in her tone would not go away.

❋

For the rest of the year the house resounded with classical music from noon till dusk. When she was not practising music, she would listen to recordings, or concentrate on DVDs of well-known singers.

Conversation between Khalid and Sultana became occasional and perfunctory. Even her moments with their son were hostage to the demands of music. Khalid filled in the gaps by explaining to the boy that his mother's singing brought joy to many people.

Khalid had been caught unawares. He was not prepared for this moment. He had to admit that his wife's was no ordinary talent. Her presentation had a special flavour that only the temperament and persona of an instinctive raag vocalist could bring to a piece. He was at a loss as to how to deal with something that seemed to have a life of its own.

Whenever he came across Khalid, Ustaad Maratab Ali had the unfortunate habit of dwelling on Sultana's skills.

'She has progressed from film music to ghazals, from pure classicism to spiritual music.'

Khalid nodded uneasily, not knowing where this was leading.

'If she seems distant,' Maratab Ali continued, 'it's because she is captive to her art. When the fusion of her soul with the spirit of music is complete, she'll return to you.'

The word 'captive' jarred on Khalid. He was about to tell Maratab Ali to keep his views to himself, but held back.

One morning, Khalid's conference with the bank auditors was interrupted by Sultana's message on his cellphone: 'Important matter to discuss.'

'What do you want to talk about, Sulti?' he asked when he got home, assuming that it may have something to do with their son's birthday party that evening.

'I've been invited to perform a *milaad* at the inauguration of the First Family Bank complex.'

'A *milaad* … in public…'

'Yes … in praise of the Prophet.'

'But, Sulti, the banking fraternity is likely to be there.'

'Does that matter when the cause is worthy?'

Spotting her well-rounded figure at the function draped in a sari instead of the customary salwar kameez, Khalid felt put out. Unlike her earlier recitals at select gatherings of friends and acquaintances, this was her first public appearance. With her head covered, she sat on a dais – flanked by her accompanists – poised, awaiting her cue. It came, after a *tilawat* from the Quran.

Khalid looked away before she started a *naat* in praise of the Prophet. He found the experience unsettling. The curious glances of the bankers added to his discomfort. A word of thanks by the presiding official in his concluding remarks to 'Madam' Sultana was the last straw. Khalid's boss's comments on the *milaad* being 'very moving and Sultana's tonation, perfect' brought no relief.

'Sulti,' Khalid said, when they got home, 'if you're going to do this professionally, what name do you intend to use?'

She thought for a while. 'Why, my own, of course – Sultana Jahan.'

'What about Hassan, where did that go?'

'Well, I attended the inauguration for a *naat* recital, not as Mrs Khalid Hassan.'

'Isn't that a kind of annulment?' Khalid asked in an undertone.

'Nonsense! People attending my performances will want to hear my voice … won't matter whether or not I'm married.'

'Isn't there some problem about priority there?'

'Khalid, you're not getting the point. Of course, marriage is important, I'm Mrs Khalid Hassan socially, and I love it. But my vocation is also part of me ... the essential me ... like ... like the bank is part of you ... we share a life together ... yet, surely, each of us has a right to our own space.'

The *milaad* was succeeded by TV recitals of the *marsiya*, to mark the month of Muharram. The recitals gave way to ghazal performances at which she delighted audiences with renderings of verses from Amir Khusrao to Faiz Ahmed Faiz. As Sultana's fame spread, she was dubbed 'Queen of ghazal'.

Another day, another sms set Khalid on edge, wondering what she had in mind. He found her waiting impatiently at home.

'You've put up with my demands for long,' she said, 'so I feel it's time to pay my way.'

'What do you want to do *now*?'

'Well, I'm making more money than you. So I should bear the cost of my musicians and equipment ... and ... of course ... compensate you for what you've spent on my music.'

Before he could think of a fitting response, there was a call from the State Guest House to remind her of the time fixed for her performance at a banquet that evening in honour of the Chinese President.

For the third time on a Sunday morning following the banquet, the upper register of Sultana's voice gathered momentum, allowing her to hold on to an elusive note, edging towards a coda. Then there was silence and the musical accompaniment ground to a halt.

Woken up over the weekend by jarring musical notes, Khalid struggled out of bed, making unsteadily for the balustrade. He saw their son sitting cross-legged on the landing, peering at the scene below.

'For God's sake, Sulti,' Khalid called downstairs, 'can't you make this infernal din later in the day?'

Caught in mid-flow, mouth wide open, Sultana looked up at him and all but choked.

'I'm sorry … we disturbed you … but my debut in classical music at the National Music Conference is a few days away. Ustaad insists on several practice sessions.'

Khalid wished he had put his foot down when it mattered. It was too late now to stop her. Her appearance at the concert had been televised, publicized in the press, billed across town on giant hoardings as a not-to-be-missed crossover from ghazal to classical music. So he relented, resigned to music at weekends.

'Okay, Sulti, but keep the decibels down.'

She recommenced with gusto. He could not help noticing the sinuous movements, poised hand, twirling fingers, the musicians bent over instruments, squatting in a semicircle around her, exclaiming 'wah' after each phrase.

It struck him that a transition had taken place.

Sultana was no longer just a housewife but a rather more significant entity.

The concert at the National Music Conference proved to be a turning point for Sultana.

On getting home at two in the morning after the concert, she was surprised to find Khalid in the alcove in the dark.

'What're you doing here, jani?'

'Waiting for you, Sulti.'

'What for?'

'I wanted a few words.'

'But you could've spoken to me in the morning?'

'Getting your attention during the day isn't easy,' he said with a laugh.

'Well then,' she said, sitting down and patting the seat next to her, 'what is it?'

'We got married for love, Sulti, music was not part of the deal.'

Tensing, she said, 'What're you getting at?'

'Love and marriage have been replaced by music in our home.'

'That,' she sputtered, 'that's an awful thing to say.'

'Is it? Where, my darling, do I, or our son, rank?'

'You're both the dearest things on earth ... I'd be lost without you.'

'No, Sulti, music is your life, we're bystanders.'

'Khalid,' Sultana said, panic in her voice, 'don't ask

me to give up music. It's God's gift ... please don't force impossible choices on me.'

'I'd never do that. What chance do even the dearest things on earth have against God's gift? Music is within ... you're driven ... you can't help it ... but I do expect you to find the right balance between that and us before you lose more than you bargained for.'

That was the last time Khalid and Sultana spoke on the subject.

❀

In the years that followed, Sultana drew audiences from the world over. Her earlier performances though had met with a mixed response. Her style was not to everyone's liking. It was individual, eclectic. Occasionally, an arrangement of notes regarded as unalterable by musical tradition was adapted to suit Sultana's vocalization.

Professional rivals, structure purists and vested interests were provoked to protect their turf. They were fiercely critical. But her artistry surmounted the onslaught. She was ultimately acknowledged as a leading exponent of both ghazal and raag.

Khalid sensed that her life had developed its own momentum. Something bigger than them had taken over. His presence in her life was marginal. She was someone lesser beings would have to watch and serve.

e other side of the footlights. He
ving her on foreign concert tours
 an intruder in her 'musical family'.
their son's devotion for Sultana had
er preference for music.

ravelled for a concert recital, she felt
nt of holding an audience enthralled
experience, one she could not quite
of power underlined by humility … the
n the face of triumph.

also took its toll. Loneliness dogged her.
she woke up with a pain in her chest and did
what to attribute it to. She felt frightened and
it had only herself to blame.

On returning from performance tours, Sultana would go into retreat. After one such tour, exhausted and wrung out, she stayed away from the public for almost three months.

'What's the matter, Sulti?' Khalid asked.

'I don't know … need to re-invent myself. I no longer feel the urge to work. Perhaps the desire has gone…'

Dear God, he thought, *is it possible*?

But then, there was a phone call from Mumbai which she answered, albeit reluctantly.

The next day she left for India to take part in 'a newly

conceptualized concert by Coke S[...]
production values'.

Her replies from Mumbai to Khali[...] [...] erratic and confused. She seemed to b[...] truth, she was missing her family. Sh[...] and her son, but could not get round [...]

'Don't worry, Sulti. All will go we[...] her. 'It always does, 'cause you're the [...]

On the opening night, Khalid and[...] down to watch a live telecast of the conce[...] Stadium in aid of the World Disaster Relie[...]

Strobe lights criss-crossed by multicolo[...] beams and myriad rays darting from numer[...] raked over a multitudinous audience throngi[...] sides of a luminous stage. The backdrop [...] fifteen-feet-high letters forming the words 'CO[...] STUDIO PRESENTS, SYNTHESIS'. The phrase also blazed intermittently across the skyline, lighting up the stadium.

In her dressing room, Sultana looked at her reflection. She was appalled by what she saw. Tears flowed unchecked, streaking across her make-up.

This image is not mine, she sobbed. *It's what's left of Sulti … not wife or mother … only a hollow presence.*

As Khalid puzzled over Sultana's role in this bizarre setting, a popular Bollywood celebrity bounced on stage and announced, 'Globalization has become our way of

music. The sound seemed to come from somewhere within.

Fragments of the fading sun filtered through veranda windows. In the twilight setting of the alcove, Khalid spotted his son, rapt, reciting the scales to the hum of the tanpura.

The youthful timbre of the boy's voice had the unmistakeable tone of a budding vocalist.

Tears gleaming in the corners of Khalid's eyes were belied by the smile playing on his lips.

Queen's Garden

Krishan Kumar seemed to have spent most of his life surrounded by vegetables. His mother delivered him in a cauliflower patch. Later, he had lain in her lap when she sat cross-legged at street corners selling fresh greens, or slept in an improvised hammock suspended from an awning under which she displayed tomatoes, cucumbers and peppers.

By the age of five, he had been initiated into the world of Empress Market where he helped his father unload trucks of farm produce from Sabzi Mandi and deliver basket loads to retailers.

Krishan was fascinated by the sights, sounds and smells of what was the food supply centre of the city. He spent hours wandering through its labyrinthine interiors. A kind tally clerk took him under his wing, teaching him to read and write.

Krishan picked up the intricacies of the vegetable trade by observing retailers. When old enough, he bid for a stall with wages saved over the years. He called the outlet Queen's Garden after Victoria, patron of the market.

The toothless grin on his father's face at the opening of the stall was a magical moment for Krishan. The old man belonged to the dwindling population of Hindus who had stayed on after their homeland became part of Pakistan.

'It's a big thing,' the tally clerk pointed out to a butcher, 'for a Hindu to be accepted in the food supply business by the Muslim groups who control it.'

'We're traders, not bigots,' the butcher commented. 'Besides, Krishan is one of us, he's a decent fellow … honest and fair … gets on well with everyone … wholesalers … retailers … local administration … political parties, mafias.'

Krishan lived in a chawl that was part of a Hindu trust. It was situated near Guru Mandir. His parents had lived there since British colonial days. After they died, only Krishan and his wife were left. Their offspring were stillborn.

❀

Every day at dawn Krishan rode his bike to Sabzi Mandi to purchase vegetables. The fresh stock was delivered in time for the opening of Empress Market at 9.

Regular customers turned up at Queen's Garden during morning hours. Bulk purchasers like hotels, clubs and hospitals placed orders in the afternoon.

Others, like foreign embassies and bargain hunters, drawn by the freshness and reasonable price of his goods, came in the evening. By 9 p.m., when the market closed, Krishan's assistants would have disposed of remnants and cleaned the stall.

Krishan attended to the 'regulars' personally. He was familiar with their preferences, idiosyncrasies and haggling. He had his 'special' and 'dreaded' clients.

One of his favourites was an olive-skinned girl who maintained a purchase account with him. He was taken by her brown eyes and dimpled smile when she first visited Queen's Garden looking for bay leaves, coriander, coconut, onion seeds and cherry peppers. She returned often, asking for the same items – a must, it seemed, for Goan cuisine.

Krishan was especially wary of a grey-bearded maulana who came daily to make purchases for his madrassa. The maulana was invariably accompanied by three teenage Pathan students carrying baskets bulging with provisions. Krishan knew that the maulana dealt with him in preference to Muslim stallholders because his rates were negotiable. Faith, he came to realize, did not stand in the way of commercial shrewdness.

While the maulana ordered carrots, potatoes,

tomatoes and greens, the students stood two steps behind him. They were uniformly capped and clad in grey salwar kameez. Eyes lowered, they did not speak unless addressed by the maulana in Pashto – and acted only in response to his instructions.

One of them was somewhat different. He looked older than the others. He was taller and had a fine growth of golden hair on his upper lip and cheeks. Krishan caught him looking up on a few occasions. When by chance their glances met, the blue-green eyes lowered immediately.

❉

On returning to the madrassa one morning, the maulana told the older boy to deliver the provisions to the kitchen. 'After that, Amanullah,' he said, 'it's your turn to hang the weekly laundry to dry … you can join classes later.'

'Yes, maulana sahib,' the boy murmured, eyes downcast, turning to go.

Amanullah hung the soggy laundry on nylon ropes crisscrossing the roof. Openings between the flapping clothes revealed glimpses of the adjacent building. While fastening wet items with pegs, he saw something through an open window for the first time – a young girl undressing and taking a shower, her nakedness glistening in the morning light.

He felt the blood rise to his temples. His hair stood on end. He felt constriction in the chest, a stirring near the backbone and extraordinary turbulence within, followed by a numbing sense of relief.

Gasping, he ran downstairs to the hammam hoping to wash the unusual experience out of his system. Later, he crept into class where students were memorizing tables. He tried to concentrate on passages earmarked by the ustaad, but lost focus when vivid images flashed by. Overcome by guilt, he put the books away and stood up to leave.

'Where're you going Amanullah?' the ustaad asked.

'I … don't feel well … please excuse me, sir.'

For two days Amanullah lay in bed wrestling with his conscience. He could differentiate between acceptable sexual conduct and prohibited deeds. He had been warned about Satan's lurking presence. But he had not been told how to cope with the new sensation that surged and ebbed in him.

※

On the third day, he was sent to Empress Market to buy food supplies without the maulana, who had other pressing engagements. Amnaullah followed written instructions when buying meat, rice and other staples. While waiting for the vegetables he had ordered at Queen's Garden, he looked up by chance and saw the girl approach the stall.

From that moment Amanullah seemed to be in a

trance. He followed her into the bus for Ranchore Lines. On getting there, he dogged her steps through narrow streets. From a cul-de-sac three leather-jacketed motorcyclists suddenly roared out encircling the terrified girl. One sang in a twangy voice, 'Maria ... Maria ... I just met a girl named Maria.'

Amanullah set his food baskets against a wall and catapulted on to the singer, knocking him down, toppling his startled companion as well and turning towards the third, who fled. Then he grabbed hold of the girl's hand, tugging hard, forcing her to run with him all the way to the Catholic cooperative apartment building where he first saw her. He released her at the entrance, but before she could speak, he went back to retrieve his things. Moments later, she watched him return with the baskets and enter the madrassa next door.

'Maria,' her mother called out when she got home, 'you look terrible ... what's the matter?'

'The Gonsalves boys...'

'Been bothering you again ... have they?'

'No ... no ... just rode around on motorbikes.'

'I'll speak to Father Francis.'

Maria was in a quandary for the rest of the day, wondering who her rescuer was.

In the evening she drifted into a little park that lay between her building and the madrassa. She half hoped he would come. Seminary students usually jogged or strode vigorously around the park in little groups after sunset. She sat on a bench, waiting.

He did come accompanied by two others and walked by without looking at her. After completing three rounds briskly, they went back to the madrassa.

When the park was almost empty, she decided to leave. As she neared the gate, he stepped out from behind an oleander bush and held out his hand. She took it and they walked silently to a secluded grove.

Away from prying eyes, he touched her breast. She smiled. They sat on the grass, spoke a while. As the evening wore on, they were drawn into discovering each other, making love on instinct.

It was the first time for both. After that they met again and again, in the morning at Queen's Garden and in the evening at the grove, not daring to think beyond being together.

❋

Two days before the month of Ramazan, Amanullah was picked by the maulana to join a batch of students assigned to the northern areas for training in guerrilla warfare. The group was due to leave that evening.

Amanullah was frantic. He looked for Maria at Queen's Garden, outside her building and in the park. Not finding her anywhere, he went to Krishan in desperation, startling him by giving him a note for Maria.

'I've got to go away,' Amanullah explained. 'This message is for her.'

When she came to know about his departure, she was desolate but unable to share her grief with anyone. Shortly after, she caught a fever, which lingered. Her mother took her to Holy Family Hospital, where Maria underwent a number of tests. Afterwards, the doctor told her she was pregnant. The news added to her sense of desolation, yet she had the presence of mind to plead with the doctor not to tell her mother.

'It'll kill her.'

'That's what they all say,' the doctor remarked, '*that* or … she'll kill me … Anyway, she'll have to know sooner or later … delay is not good … she may have a solution.'

'Later, doctor, please later … not now … I've got to prepare her for the news.'

A few days later, Maria decided to end the pregnancy. She thought of ways and means, of people who might help. Nothing came to mind.

She could not do this on her own. Not knowing where to turn, she went to church hoping to find some guidance. As she was about to go in, she felt nauseous. So she threw up at the entrance. She caught a glimpse of Father Francis observing her from the church gate.

It was quiet and cool inside. There was no one about. She went up to the church, and entered a pew in the nave. She sat down and prayed, hands clasped.

Her concentration was disturbed by the sound of fluttering. Looking up at the arched ceiling, she noticed pigeons near the skylight above the altar. She tried praying again but failed. Instead, she burst into tears, shoulders racked by intense sobbing. Moments later, she felt a hand on her back and heard Father Francis's voice.

'Why do you cry, my child?'

Caught unawares, she said, 'Just upset Father … no reason … really.'

The priest looked at her searchingly.

'You're keeping something back. Come with me, drink some water … wash your face … then we'll talk.'

He overcame her resistance firmly, leading the way.

In the confessional, Maria revealed the secret but would not disclose Amanullah's identity. The priest promised to talk to her parents and help with the pregnancy.

'Abortion,' he said, 'is out of the question … it's a cardinal sin.'

True to his word, Father Francis discussed the problem with the parents tactfully, shielding her from their wrath. He also arranged for her stay at a convent, until delivery.

❧

Maria found the convent peaceful. She was no longer burdened with a guilty secret. The task of coping with the pregnancy had been taken over by responsible people. She had been saved from committing the sin of abortion. The longing for Amanullah was abating a little each day.

Her primary concern was the baby's future. Her parents were prepared to take her back without the infant. She heard the nuns chatter about putting the child up for adoption by a Christian – preferably Catholic – family. A foreign childless couple would, of course, be the best option. Since she could not keep the baby, she had a girlish desire to save it for Amanullah somehow.

All other arrangements for its future seemed like abandonment to her.

The baby was born on time – a chubby, fair-haired boy with blue-green eyes. Maria was given ten days for tending her son. After that he was to be taken away to lessen the pain of separation.

On the ninth day, Maria sneaked out of the convent with the baby sleeping in a carrycot. She could not take it home, or to the madrassa. There was only one other place she could think of where she felt the child could safely wait for his father. She boarded a rickshaw for Empress Market. On the way, she recalled Krishan's merry face and the gentle way in which he handled vegetables. She remembered the care and concern with which he had given her Amanullah's note.

By the time she got there, Maria had cleaned, fed

and held the baby for the last time. She waited for the afternoon prayers to start, and then moved stealthily towards Queen's Garden.

As she had hoped, Krishan was away, probably having tea at the tally clerk's office. His assistants were at the mosque. She placed the carrycot amidst a heap of cauliflowers and left quickly, tears clouding her eyes.

Krishan spotted the carrycot the instant he got back to Queen's Garden. He peered inside and was surprised at seeing the baby. He assumed the child had been left there by accident and that someone would come looking for it. But no one came.

As the evening shadows lengthened, the baby began to stir, making mewling noises. Krishan picked it up instinctively and noticed two feeding bottles – one of milk, the other of water – in the cot. He held the baby close and fed it from the milk bottle. It soon settled down and looked up at Krishan with its blue-green eyes. He watched it nestle in his arms, suckling milk. It was his first experience at baby minding – and it came to him naturally.

'Little pumpkin,' he murmured, 'just a sweet little pumpkin.'

Then he saw a tag attached to the baby's ankle – which Maria had not removed. There was something written on it. It contained the baby's date of birth, its sex, the mother's name was given as 'Maria Fernandes', and against the word father, it said: 'Unknown.' Under that, a message written in a childish scrawl, stated, 'Krishanji, please keep the baby for his father. You know him.'

Krishan realized that the baby had been left deliberately at Queen's Garden. He thought at first of getting in touch with the Fernandes family, but changed his mind when he considered how this might affect Maria.

Since he could think of nothing else to do, he decided to take the baby home where his wife could help him attend to its needs until a better solution was found.

'How will you take care of it?' one of his assistants asked.

'As I've taken care of my vegetables all these years.'

Krishan's wife, Savitri, was reluctant at first to take the baby.

'God has put the child in our way,' he reasoned. 'It's our duty to take care of it for the time being.'

'But whose is it?'

'I found it lying among the vegetables.'

Muttering, she laid the baby on a bed and checked the contents of the carrycot. There were extra clothes, a packet of pampers and two containers of powdered milk.

'Whoever left the child, certainly provided for its survival … I suppose I'd better change its nappy.'

She brought a basinful of water and cotton wool. Krishan watched admiringly.

'No point looking at me like that,' she said, 'I do know about babies even though I'm old now … I watched my sisters with their little ones.'

She undid the baby's pamper, cleaned its genitals and bottom with damp cotton wool. She noticed that the baby was circumcised.

'It's not one of ours,' she said, pointing to its member.

'It's ours, Savitri, as long as it's with us.'

Krishan waited daily at Queen's Garden for someone to lay claim to the baby. He also checked from fellow traders at the market if anyone had come asking for a missing child. No one came.

❦

Three months later Krishan heard someone asking for bay leaves, coriander, coconut, onion seeds and cherry peppers. It was Maria's mother.

'Salam, Mrs Fernandes, good to see you … it's been a long time … how's your daughter?'

'She's gone to Canada. We were very busy with her wedding and all. Her husband's a nice Goan boy from Bombay … manages a supermarket in Toronto.'

After getting that news Krishan did not expect a mother to come looking for the baby.

❦

Amanullah returned to Karachi after two years of training and three years of manoeuvres in mountainous terrain. He had travelled back with some mujahidin who needed specialized treatment for injuries sustained in skirmishes. After settling them in the madrassa, he was under orders to return to the base camp.

'You've become a man,' the maulana said admiringly, embracing him and eyeing the impressive bearing, the flowing golden beard.

'I've tried to follow your teachings,' Amanullah said.

'What's this we hear about you being some kind of a killing machine?' asked the maulana.

'I get angry sometimes ... very angry ... at people who break God's rules,' Amanullah replied self-consciously, 'but I'm not a wild man.'

'Well, we're happy to have you here. Rest a few days before your return ... only, don't get into one of the rages you're known for.'

That evening, Amanullah was drawn to the roof. He looked once more at the window through which he had first seen Maria. He was no longer in love with her. Time, physical hardship and indoctrination had scotched all such emotions. His sexual needs were met by a teenage bride from the tribal area. He had not thought of Maria for months, yet the view from the roof aroused his interest.

He went to the park and made his way to the grove. In

the twilight, memories came flooding back. He recalled the pain and their delight in each other. Suddenly seized by fear of retribution, he rammed a fist into a tree trunk, chiding himself for reviving unclean thoughts.

Next day, he awakened for morning prayers. He spent time reading the Quran and meditating.

In the afternoon, he took a bus to Saddar, intending to call on acquaintances in downtown seminaries. For some reason, he got off near Empress Market and wandered in. His footsteps led him to Queen's Garden.

On seeing Krishan seated, as always, in the midst of his green world, it seemed that time had stopped. He looked across the stall as if expecting someone's approach. Then he glanced at Krishan awkwardly. Their eyes met, as once before. Krishan recognized the blue-green gaze of the youthful seminarian of five years ago.

He recalled too having seen it elsewhere. With a start, he recognized the look of Bilal, the little boy who had stolen the hearts of Krishan and Savitri with the ease of the Hindu deity Kanhaiya.

Krishan responded awkwardly to Amanullah's salam. Amanullah looked at him searchingly. Uncertain of what to do next, he moved away. Then he came back impulsively and asked, 'That note … I gave you some time ago … do you remember?'

Krishan realized that the moment for revelation had come.

'That note was given to the girl.'

'What happened then?'

'She left for Canada.'

'Canada ... so she has gone away.'

'Yes ... far away.'

Amanullah turned to go.

'Wait,' Krishan called before Amanullah got lost in the crowd. 'There's more.'

'What more could there be?'

'There's ... there's ... a child, a little boy, born after you left.'

'What're you talking about?' Amanullah asked with ferocity.

Krishan took Amanullah to a tea shop where he told him all.

After a long silence, Amanullah said menacingly, 'She abandoned the child and started a new life elsewhere.'

'Think of her position, a Christian girl, almost a child herself, giving birth to an illegitimate baby ... fathered by a mujahid ... in a country like Pakistan.'

'Why did she leave the child with you?'

'Who else knew the father's identity ... since she couldn't keep it ... how else could she make sure that you would have access to it?'

Amanullah got up suddenly. 'I've to think about all this ... I'll go now.'

Savitri reacted angrily when Krishan told her about the encounter with Amanullah.

'Why did you talk to him?'

'There was no other way ... the mother would expect me to do that.'

'*Expect*? What do you mean, expect?' Tears welled up in her eyes. 'Did she obtain your consent before dumping Bilal on us?'

'She did what she had to.'

'Well ... we did what we were forced to do ... now that he's become ours ... we're being made to give him up.'

'He was only ours to look after until someone with a proper claim turned up.'

'So ... we were only temporary care givers?'

'That's what God intended. And we've done our job – with honour.'

'Krishan, I ... want ... to keep him.'

'Stop, Savitri, I'm not going to commit paap where the boy's concerned.

❈

At the madrassa, the maulana listened in amazement to Amanullah's monotonic account of the episode.

'I tell you this because you're my teacher, my guide. The last few years I've sought forgiveness for the sin of fornication ... hundreds ... no ... thousands of times ...

but the existence of a child of which I didn't know is a different kind of problem...'

'The existence of a bastard, you mean,' intoned the maulana, 'a bastard born of a non-believer ... raised by non-believers.'

'Do I have any responsibility for this child of whom I knew nothing?'

'Of course, you do ... you helped create it, so you are responsible.'

'What should I do?'

'Kill it,' shrieked the maulana. 'Destroy the abomination that pollutes the world.'

'Kill the child?'

'Destroy what is abhorrent to God ... that's what a true mujahid would do.'

All night long Amanullah paced feverishly up and down the road facing the madrassa. From morning till noon he lay prostrate in the prayer chamber seeking guidance.

By late afternoon he was at Queen's Garden. Krishan was expecting him. He was puzzled by the steely look in Amanullah's eyes. Krishan suggested that Amanullah should accompany him home to see the boy. Amanullah nodded, looking straight ahead. When Krishan asked Amanullah about his plans for the boy, he did not answer.

To allay apprehension likely to be aroused by the

sight of a bearded mujahid in a Hindu chawl, Krishan had informed the inhabitants of the building that he would be accompanied by a Pathan guest. So when they walked in there were stares of curiosity, not fear.

They went up to Krishan's first-floor apartment. Savitri, head covered by her sari pallu, let them in. Amanullah was struck by the simple, clean living quarters. He also noticed the red dot on Savitri's forehead, then looked away. Tea and biscuits were served but were left untouched by Amanullah.

'You should know something about the boy before you meet him,' Krishan said.

Amanullah nodded.

'He's been brought up as a Muslim...'

'As a Muslim?' Amanullah echoed, taken unawares. 'How ... how's that possible?'

'Because that's what he is,' Krishan explained.

'Because we made it happen,' Savitri said from the kitchen.

'He was named Bilal after the first muezzin,' Krishan continued. 'He's being educated in a madrassa that teaches English, maths, and science along with Islamic studies.'

'We've observed Muslim practices with regard to feeding, bathing and clothing him,' Savitri added.

'You did all this for him ... and he's not even your child,' Amanullah remarked, visibly astonished.

'Children are God's gift to mankind. They don't ask to be born, but He sends them anyway … and so they must be cared for and nurtured by us … like … like … fresh vegetables,' Krishan said. 'Now come, let me show him to you.'

Krishan led Amanullah to the veranda running in front of the apartments from which they looked down on the quadrangle where children were playing. Bilal stood out among the children because of his fair hair. Krishan called out, asking him to come upstairs.

'Billu,' one of the children was heard saying, 'we'll wait till you get back.'

Bilal came scampering up. Seeing Amanullah's towering figure next to Krishan, he hesitated, murmured, 'Assalamalaikum' quietly, and then walked instinctively towards Savitri who stood in the doorway. He squeezed himself beside her, looking with curiosity at the two men, half screened by the pleats of her sari.

'Beta,' Krishan said, holding out his hand.

'Yes, Baba,' Bilal replied.

'Come here, I want you to meet the person I was telling you about … He was very close to your parents.'

Bilal came forward uncertainly, right hand thrust forward. Amanullah took the little hand and shook it.

'You knew my parents?' Bilal asked.

'Yes,' Amanullah replied, taken aback by a face that was new and yet so familiar. He reached out for Bilal, then stopped abruptly. Recalling that he had to kill the bastard, he steeled himself to remain firm. He released Bilal's hand abruptly and stepped back, doubling up as if in pain, assailed by a host of conflicting thoughts. He found it strange for Hindus to have raised a Muslim child. He wondered whether that was a breach of the laws of God. Stranger still, the maulana regarded Bilal as an 'abomination', yet Krishan had described children as God's gift to mankind. It came to him with a start that he was responsible for Bilal's presence – for his illegitimate status. There was no escaping the realization.

'God help me,' he moaned.

'What's the matter?' Krishan asked, concerned.

Bilal inched back towards Savitri, disturbed. He seemed anxious to get away.

'Ma,' he said, 'I want to go down and play.'

'Yes, my child,' Savitri said, 'you go and play.'

'Stop,' Amanullah cried, standing straight and holding up his hand.

Everyone froze. For a while, no one moved, blinked or even seemed to breathe. Then Amanullah doubled up again.

'Go child,' he said, 'go and play. I must leave now … I'll come back tomorrow.'

Amanullah avoided the madrassa lest he came across the maulana. He went instead to an outhouse – where the ustaad resided – to unburden himself.

'I was filled with dread when it came to killing him. I felt something's wrong. I just couldn't do it,' Amanullah said.

'I'm not going to comment on the instructions given by the maulana,' the ustaad said, 'but from the texts, I've learnt that deliberate killing of an innocent person in peacetime for a flaw for which he's not responsible, is forbidden.'

'What am I to do then?' Amanullah asked.

'There are no rules to guide us in these circumstances ... except the ones applicable by analogy ... and logic. Now let's see ... the child's yours ... you cannot legitimize him by marrying the mother because she's gone away and probably married another. It's your duty to raise the child ... so ... take him back with you anyway ... you've a wife at home and – God willing – you'll have children of her in due course ... who'll regard this child as their big brother.'

As promised, Amanullah went again to Queen's Garden. Krishan looked up and knew why he had come.

'It's today isn't it?' Krishan asked.

Amanullah nodded.

'I've prepared Bilal for it, but please be patient with him ... we've looked after him like our own.'

'I could see that. What do I owe you for taking care of the child?'

'What do you mean ... money for raising Bilal?'

Krishan bristled. 'Don't ... don't reduce what we did ... to .... to a trade.'

'But how can I repay you?'

'By caring for him as we've done.'

At Krishan's apartment there was sadness. A resigned Savitri waited for the inevitable to happen. Bilal, bewildered and benumbed, sat on his suitcase, waiting for his world to crumble. When the men came, they were met with silence.

'Come, Bilal,' Krishan said, hoping to avoid a prolonged farewell, 'your father's here to take you home.'

Bilal got up, slung the strap of his schoolbag over his shoulder and moved stiffly towards Amanullah. Amanullah held out his hand. Bilal took it. Krishan picked up the suitcase.

'I'll walk with you to the bus stop,' Krishan said, 'but Bilal, first say goodbye to your ma.'

Bilal wrenched his hand from Amanullah's grasp and ran to Savitri. She gathered him in her arms, fought back tears and kissed him repeatedly. Then she pushed him away forcibly, almost as if she were detaching a limb, and retreated swiftly to the kitchen.

'Here, you'd better take the suitcase,' Krishan said to Amanullah, his voice choking, 'so that I can carry him to the terminus. You can see he's in no condition to walk all the way there.'

It dawned on Amanullah that an uprooted plant did

not always thrive in alien soil. Then glancing at Krishan reassuringly, he straightened up and said, 'Let me carry him.'

Krishan nodded. Amanullah picked up Bilal. When their faces were level, he looked into the depths of his son's blue-green eyes and held him close. It seemed to Amanullah that he was looking deep inside himself.

'Are we going home?' Bilal asked wearily.

'You *are* home,' Amanullah said.

He set Bilal down, turned and walked away, looking straight ahead.

Bilal watched him go, wondering whether he would ever get to see his father's blue-green world.

The Misfits

Adnan Rafiq landed in Islamabad the day Zafar Langha started work as personal assistant to Kunwar Rafiq Ahmed, Adnan's father. Having graduated as Juris Doctor from the Harvard Law School, Adnan was returning home after three years. He was met by his mother, Shabana, and older sister, Farah, escorted by an official. The uneasiness he felt during the flight gave way to mixed emotions when he saw them.

Shabana sported bleached curls, toreador pants, a youngish kurta – which failed to conceal bulges – and a trailing scarf.

'Wow,' he remarked, putting an arm around her flirtatiously, 'you always manage to surprise me.' He recalled too well her visits to cosmetology clinics on her trips to the US.

'You like it?' she asked in broad Punjabi intonation, flicking her scarf. 'But your sister doesn't.'

'Farah's got no taste,' he said, winking at his sensibly clad sister. They hugged warmly. The official took Adnan's passport and baggage tags for processing. 'I see, I'm getting VIP treatment,' Adnan said.

'Islamabad is a VIP sanctuary,' Farah said, 'brimming with ministers, parliamentarians, generals – prime targets for suicide bombers.'

Adnan smiled, then asked, 'Where's Papa?'

'New secretary's first day at work,' Shabana said.

'Special Personal Assistant, Mama,' Farah corrected.

'Your Papa is important man … you know,' Shabana said smugly.

'And where's Shabby's … I mean … Mama's little lamb?' Adnan asked, alluding to his younger brother, Tariq.

'Still calling me by silly name,' Shabana remarked peevishly. 'Have respect for your mother.'

'Sorry dearest, you know how it is … I feel you're more our generation than Papa's.'

Shabana did not know how to take that. Farah giggled.

'Where else would lambkins be but hanging out with his flashy mates? "A"-level failures preparing for a re-sit,' Farah said.

'Tariq, you're talking about, he's having tuition for final paper,' Shabana explained, ignoring Farah.

'He's doing more than that,' Farah said in low tones. 'He's in the fast track – cars, girls, underground music scene, drugs and booze – all in the Islamic Republic.'

The official returned and shepherded them to a four-wheel-drive Land Cruiser.

'My, my,' Adnan remarked, taking in the turbaned driver, armed guards, escort vehicle, 'we've gone up in the world.'

'And how,' Farah murmured.

❦

Zafar Langah was anxious to succeed in his first job in Islamabad as Kunwar's SPA. Kunwar was something of an icon for natives of the rural Punjab backwater – Zafar's home – as the first local to achieve such prominence in government.

'Rafiq', for that was how he was referred to in earlier days – the prefix 'Kunwar' being a later addition, a socially elevating one – had started his career as a patwari with the local administration, collecting agricultural tax for government revenue accounts. He had served under Zafar's father, who, as tehsildar, supervised the activities of the patwaris.

Zafar had turned down a job opportunity with a multinational organization that financed poverty alleviation programmes, in favour of Kunwar's offer. He was thrilled at being selected from seventy-eight applicants for the post, owing to his skills in accountancy and English language.

'Rare to find a local graduate so competent in both the subjects,' Kunwar had written on Zafar's portfolio.

The remark had prompted Zafar to pray for a special place in heaven for the Christian missionary who had tutored him privately. Had his learning been confined to the derelict local school, he would have floundered, like some of his schoolmates. Nor would he have got into the accountancy course in which he had excelled.

When his father heard about the job, he pumped the air joyfully. 'Learn all you can from Rafiq,' he advised Zafar, 'his way is *the way* to success for persons of our class in this country. But always be respectful, humble ... never disclose your relationship with me. Never, never remind him of his origins ... nor his association with this area.'

✳

Zafar was let in at the entrance to Kunwar's home – after being frisked by a guard – just as the Land Cruiser turned into a paved driveway leading through a picturesque garden to a house designed in the style of an Abu Dhabi 'Sheikh' residence.

Adnan and Zafar looked briefly at each other.

'Who's that?' Adnan asked.

'Special Assistant, I guess,' Farah said, shrugging her shoulders.

Going through the massive entrance to the house, Adnan stopped, eyes blinking. 'Gosh,' he said, 'straight out of Bollywood.'

Taking in the chandeliers, carvings, circular staircase, and a profusion of objects signifying 'no money spared', he wondered how he would fit into such a milieu. Sensing resignation in Farah's attitude, he assumed the opulence had dulled her senses.

Magnificent, thought Zafar, gawking at the surroundings, as he was led down a corridor to the office wing by a rotund man of middle years who introduced himself as 'Munshiji'. *It's like ... so like ... a movie set. Never dreamt I'd be working in such a place.*

❧

Kunwar Rafiq was waiting anxiously for his son in the living room. When they came in, he murmured an incantation.

'Prayers answered,' he continued, unable to take his eyes off a handsome twenty-four-year-old version of himself. He embraced Adnan warmly, stepped back to take another look, breathing fast.

'You look wonderful, Mashallah. You've come home to a great future. Major law firms are expecting you to join them. You can take your pick. I'll discuss my plans for you later – at dinner – perhaps,' he said in one breath.

'Let's wait a bit, Papa,' Adnan said, somewhat unsettled by his father's exuberance. 'I need time to get my bearings. It's been three years, you know. So many questions … everything's so new … so different…'

'You're rushing him, Papa,' Farah said. 'There'll be plenty of time to discuss his future.'

Tea was served by uniformed staff, in garish Chinaware, in an alcove furnished with minimalist Scandinavian settees.

The zooming of a car on the driveway followed by screeching brakes marked the homecoming of Tariq Rafiq, shadowed by a gunman. A strapping eighteen-year-old, Tariq was more a man of the world than Adnan. The brothers embraced with measured enthusiasm. Adnan felt the old camaraderie missing – supplanted by an unspoken gulf. At a sign from Tariq, the gunman retreated.

'What's this?' Adnan asked playfully. 'A replay of the Wild West, Pakistani style?'

Before an embarrassed Tariq could respond, Shabana said, 'He needs protection from crook element.'

Tariq made some excuse about essential revision work for missing out on his brother's arrival. Farah and Adnan exchanged glances and continued munching sandwiches.

Adnan was overwhelmed by the trappings of what was now his home. Between enquiries about the trip and other small talk, he felt the uneasiness return like a lump in his throat. He guessed that not raising matters bothering him now would leave few opportunities for doing so after he was drawn into the system.

'When I left three years ago, Papa was assistant deputy secretary in the Ministry of Agriculture,' he said with a suddenness that caused a ripple, 'and we lived happily, it seemed, in a grade II government bungalow in Sector G ... and now all this. How did it happen?'

Uneasy silence followed the question that had never been asked before.

'Well,' Kunwar remarked, taken unawares, 'well ... well ... you see I'm now principal secretary, Ministry of Finance, and chief secretary of the Cabinet Division.'

'That much I know. But that doesn't explain this ... this affluence.'

The turn in conversation evoked different reactions in the others. Kunwar was disturbed by the innuendo in Adnan's queries. Shabana was piqued by his inquisitorial tone. Farah aroused, waiting to join the fray, eyes darting from father to son. Tariq showed concern for his father and creeping disapproval of his brother. All trace of conviviality was gone.

'I get a much higher salary and allowances now,' Kunwar explained reassuringly.

'Come on, Papa, that's not enough to cover all this … this … *shaan*,' Adnan said, his arms raised, indicating the surroundings, 'not to mention the four-wheel drive and armed escort.'

'Plus five other cars – including one for me and one for Tariq,' interjected Farah.

Shabana placed a restraining hand on Farah. 'Why you are asking these things?' she enquired.

'Yes. Why?' Tariq asked testily.

'He wants to know how we've become so wealthy while he's been away,' Farah remarked.

'We have lands in Khanpur,' Kunwar murmured lamely.

'Since when?' Adnan asked. 'I thought you were one of several shareholders in a small block.'

'Never,' muttered Tariq.

'No, no, my grandfather had some dower land which was in dispute for many years,' Kunwar said. 'It was finally settled in my favour.'

'Imagine!' Farah remarked. 'All 2,200 acres of prime land … lucky Papa.'

'Farah, enough now,' Shabana cautioned.

'You should be grateful, Baji,' Tariq said, 'instead of putting Papa down all the time.'

But Farah was unstoppable. 'Papa, tell him about your joint ventures in pharmaceuticals, shipping, sugar, textiles…'

'What!' Adnan remarked, visibly disturbed by the revelations.

'You see, my son,' Kunwar said tugging his left earlobe, 'as I rose in service, I was given opportunities to participate in commercial enterprises.'

'How? You'd have to invest, or be gifted shares, in them.'

Kunwar looked at his wife helplessly.

'Bank borrowings and loans from friends...' she put in.

'You're telling me that Papa's a net debtor?'

'Not ... not really,' Kunwar said, 'you see ... the businesses have done very well, thank god, and I've been able to set off the debts against the returns.'

'There,' Tariq said sitting back, 'satisfied now, Bhaijan?'

'Yes, Tariq,' Adnan said drily, 'very satisfied with the knowledge that a bureaucrat's secret to success here is to rise high enough to get loans for buying lucrative stock.'

There was a pregnant silence. At last, Adnan drew out an edition of the *Christian Science Monitor* from his hand baggage and flung it on a table facing his father.

'Oh! Papa,' he said, thumping the paper, 'why do we curse the US when its press states the truth about us?' He was alluding to an article headlined 'Pakistan's bureaucracy – a veritable quagmire of corruptocracy'.

'Or the Brits?' he went on, waving an edition of the *New Statesman*, 'who describe our administration as Ali Baba and the 400,000 thieves ... while Transparency International says we are on our way to becoming the most corrupt country in the world. I'd hoped against hope,' he continued in low tones, 'that you were not one of them.'

'What do you mean?' Kunwar bristled, jumping up from the settee. Tariq came to his father's side instinctively.

'Enough Papa ... no more now,' Adnan said, turning away from Kunwar. 'I'm tired ... want to go to my room. Farah can show me the way.'

'What about lunch?' Shabana asked.

'I think I'll skip lunch ... get some sleep instead. We'll talk later, may be at dinner.'

❁

For Zafar, Kunwar's office represented grandeur – polished wooden floors, wood panelled walls with occasional book-lined shelves, moss-green leatherette and rose-hued teak desk with a large swivel chair in tan-brown suede. A Chinese carpet separated the desk from a three-piece green leather seating arrangement. Ceiling lights and glowing lamps set strategically offset the cave-like darkness caused by lowered window blinds. A room next to the office was fitted with steel cabinets, telex, telefax, computer and a small desk intended for Zafar.

'This is where the secretary sits,' Munshi pointed out. The secretary's room led to another L-shaped room, occupied by an elderly clerk, attending to the EPABX and a younger person who was busy with files.

'Burhan sahib and Abid,' Munshi said, gesturing towards them, 'will work with you.'

Zafar's curiosity about Munshi's job abated somewhat when Munshi mentioned that he was Kunwar's 'odd-job man'. 'For all official and unofficial work,' he added with an air of mystery.

'You and I'll be working together on some matters,' he added, nudging Zafar. 'Now wait here until Kunwar sahib comes. He'll explain your work routine. At present he's at a family reunion … his elder son has returned from America.' With that, Munshi turned and waddled out of the room.

There was a brief pause. Abid offered to run Zafar through the filing cabinets. Zafar suggested that could wait until he had received Kunwar sahib's instructions.

Zafar settled in the secretary's room and occupied himself with the word processor. He was still working at it when Kunwar walked into the office.

'Zafar Langha,' he called out, 'come in here.'

Zafar got up nervously, smoothed his shirt and tie

before going in. Kunwar was standing by the swivel chair. He was tall and imposing, his aquiline features moustached and bordered by a cropped beard which was colour rinsed brown-black. Zafar bade him salaam in traditional mode.

'So you've come from the interior of Punjab to work in the capital.' Kunwar said, sitting down and motioning Zafar to a visitor's chair at the desk.

'Yes, sir,' Zafar said hurriedly to forestall further references to his background.

'Well, the work here is not regular stuff handled by secretarial staff. It calls for utmost secrecy. You must not discuss it with anyone unless instructed by me. Also, you will not disclose details of office work to anyone. If you do, you'll have to answer for it. I need your word that you'll abide by this,' Kunwar said, placing a Quran on the desk.

Zafar was nonplussed by the unusual initiation to the working arrangement. He reacted reflexively by touching the Quran and mumbling an oath to maintain secrecy about office affairs.

He was also required to sign a pledge of secrecy on stamp paper.

'Although you will be employed by me – not by the government – such precautions are necessary because of my official status,' Kunwar explained.

Zafar nodded, eyes lowered.

'You'll be working for me in a private capacity but the work may relate to personal or official matters.'

After a pause Zafar ventured to enquire about his functions.

'Specialized attendance,' Kunwar remarked, 'you'll have to deal with correspondence on commercial matters under my instructions – acknowledgments, responses and filing – also bookkeeping of special accounts identified alphabetically. Burhan will guide you.'

Zafar nodded again, not quite sure what he was meant to do.

'Your CV shows that you've worked elsewhere. Tell me about your professional experience.'

'Yes, sir. My first job was with Khanpur Sugar Mills in the accounts department. Later I joined Carson's Trading Group as secretary to the CEO.

'Impressive … this is not a high-profile post, but there's plenty to do and rewards to follow.'

'Sir, I left my last job because I preferred working for you.'

'I see,' Kunwar said, getting up to leave, 'we'll take good care of you. Burhan will show you the ropes.'

He left as swiftly as he had come.

❀

Burhan did show Zafar the ropes, or at least enough of them for Zafar to work with. He was given several ledgers identifiable by different combinations of letters. He had to enter figures in them abstracted by Burhan from statements brought by Munshi periodically. There was no indication of the enterprises to which the figures related. Most of the ledger entries constituted rupee currency figures, but some represented US dollars, the euro and the Japanese yen. The books on foreign currency operations merely required revenue and disbursement entries. Payments were made routinely to various colours, such as 'red', 'blue', 'green' and other shades.

Burhan mentioned cryptically that the coded references were necessary for maintaining confidentiality about national assets overseen by the Ministry of Finance. Zafar accepted Burhan's explanation about the ledgers, but failed, at first, to understand why he was also required to draft Kunwar's correspondence. The reason became clear when he saw samples of Kunwar's writing. It was the work of someone who had a poor grasp of English.

Zafar got accustomed to the office routine within a few days. Munshi would sidle in frequently, wink and nod at Zafar, then go into a huddle with Burhan. Zafar received Kunwar's instructions directly or routed via Burhan. Kunwar spent most of his time at the Ministry of Finance, yet made it a point to communicate regularly over telephone with his employees. Zafar could tell that Kunwar was satisfied with his work.

❄

Adnan was inducted as an associate in the Attorney General's law firm. It was a plum position for a newcomer. Kunwar had played his hand well. Despite Adnan's misgivings about his father, he felt that the best way to chart an independent course was by achieving quick success in the legal profession.

While the Attorney General was duty-bound to act as counsel for the state in government initiated prosecutions, the law firm – which handled his private practice – was run, during his term of office, by his partners, headed by Murtaza Naqvi. Naqvi had passed on some of the choicest legal briefs for study and preliminary attendance to Adnan.

They were mainly criminal matters: bribery and corruption, implicating government functionaries; scams involving state land and small tenancies by government contractors; destruction of forests by powerful feudals; bungling of oil purchase contracts by state authorities; mismanagement of state-owned corporations by political appointees and embezzlement of funds from state accounts.

The lawyer in Adnan was fascinated by the legal implications of the briefs, but at a personal level he was appalled at the enormity of the misdeeds and the prominence of those involved.

'We're acting for the defendants in all these matters,' Naqvi explained. 'We have to coordinate our court appearances carefully with the AG.'

'Why?' Adnan asked.

'Because he is state prosecutor, and we, defence counsel. So we can't appear in court in the same matter on opposite sides. That would cause a conflict of interest.'

'Odd that he should accept the post of AG when his firm is handling so many matters on behalf of persons accused of offences against the state.'

'He didn't want the job, but was pressured into accepting it by the PM. Anyway that's how it works here. For us, such cases are very lucrative. So under the current arrangement, we will act for the defendants in all those cases in which some government prosecutor other than the AG represents the state, while the AG has made it a point to avoid prosecuting those cases in which we – his firm – appear for the defence.'

'So we serve the interests of both sides.'

'Not quite "we", the AG maybe.'

'A bit like eating the cake and having it.'

❀

Shortly after Adnan had started work, Kunwar called and asked him to return home early one evening.

'Special occasion,' he explained.

When Adnan got home, preparations were under way for a high tea. Servants attended to finishing touches. A colourfully dressed Shabana fluttered over floral arrangements. Tariq stood by to help. Kunwar appeared periodically, nervously checking if all was in order.

'The governor of Punjab is coming with wife, son and relatives,' Kunwar explained.

'What for? Adnan asked.

'They're coming to see Farah,' Shabana said.

'To see Farah ... why?'

'For making marriage proposal,' Shabana said.

'Marriage,' Adnan remarked, astonished, 'to whom?'

'The son ... of course,' Tariq answered.

'Does Farah know about this?'

'Of course, silly,' Shabana said, 'also she'll be joining us.'

Just then the guard at the gate called on the intercom to say that the governor's convoy had arrived.

'Go up and change office wear for smart salwar kameez like Tariq's,' Shabana directed.

When Adnan returned, the tea was in progress. The governor, plump, red-faced and jolly-looking, was cracking mildly ribald jokes in Punjabi with Kunwar. Shabana sat with the governor's wife, who was dressed inappropriately in sunflower yellow. Chatting with Shabana did not deter her from casting sly glances at Kunwar's family members. Farah, somewhat elaborately dressed, sat stiffly on a sofa, head covered, eyes downcast. Tariq shared the sofa. The governor's son, clear-eyed and cleft-chinned, sat in a settee on Farah's left. The young men were conversing with each other across Farah's silence. Other persons in the governor's party were scattered around the room.

'Why did you keep this from me?' Adnan asked Farah after the visitors had gone.

'It was up in the air for a while, so I thought nothing of it. Believe me, the gathering today was as much a surprise for me as it was for you,' she said.

'So what happens now?'

'We'll have to wait and see whether they take the bait,' Tariq interjected, sauntering up to them.

'Don't be crude, Tariq,' Farah said.

'What's crude about that? Didn't they come to check you out?'

'That's your way of putting it,' Farah retorted.

'My way, your way, it's the traditional way. I just hope they liked you. It would be great for us to be linked with them.'

'What's so special about being linked to the governor?' Adnan asked.

'His family's one of oldest ... descended from the rulers of Awadh. Marriage with them would be great for the social image.'

'Go away, Tariq. You disgust me,' Farah said.

'Is it true? Is that why Pa and Shabby were in a tizzy?' Adnan asked.

'Well, you know how status conscious they are,' Farah said nervously.

'What about you? Why did you agree to this charade? Why didn't … Javed … if that's his name, take you on dates, or something … then propose?' Adnan enquired.

'We observe traditional forms in such matters,' Tariq said edgily.

'Don't be so stuffy' Adnan remarked.

'Stop it, you two,' Farah said. 'This concerns me more than either of you.'

'How can you consider marrying someone you don't know?' Adnan asked.

'But I do know him. We were in the same college,' Farah said.

'So you're old sweethearts then,' Adnan remarked.

'Bhaijan, you're insulting Baji,' Tariq said.

'And you're being sanctimonious,' Adnan responded.

'We're not sweethearts. I knew Javed slightly. He's okay. And Tariq's right, we do fall back on form, especially when a girl in our set-up reaches twenty-six, has no firm prospects of marriage, and has parents hell-bent on scaling the social ladder,' Farah said, walking away.

Later that evening, Shabana rushed into Farah's room, out of breath, to tell her that the governor's wife was on the phone suggesting a follow-up visit the next day for tendering a formal proposal of marriage.

'Well, darling, what'll we say to them about the proposal?' she asked. 'Not now of course. After two days, maybe.'

'Yes,' said Farah firmly. 'Yes … yes … yes … say yes … tomorrow or two days later, it doesn't matter.'

Shabana was taken aback by Farah's response, but decided not to comment. She dashed off excitedly to inform Kunwar and the boys.

❀

Farah kept twisting the slightly loose solitaire on her finger as she made her way to Kunwar's office. She was looking for a book on human rights. Hearing noises, Zafar went in to check. Both were taken by surprise.

'I'm Farah. I live here. I'm looking for a book,' she said in Urdu.

'Bibi, my name is Zafar Langha. I'm Kunwar sahib's assistant,' he responded in English.

'Of course, I saw you at the gate when we were returning from the airport after picking up my brother.'

'That was my first day on the job.'

'Do you like working here?'

Taken aback by the directness of the query, Zafar paused, then said, 'It's an honour to work for Kunwar sahib. Who wouldn't appreciate it?'

'I see,' Farah said, moving between shelves. 'My father is lucky to have such loyalty, but what about the work? Do you find it interesting?'

'Looking after national assets is an interesting task.'

'National assets?' Farah queried. 'But I thought you were a personal assistant, looking after his private interests.'

'Logging returns and disbursements of national assets is very important work. Kunwar sahib prefers to monitor such matters.'

Farah was puzzled by his response, but decided to drop the subject. Zafar realized – a little too late – that he had been indiscreet in discussing office work with Farah.

He was about to return to his room but stopped when Farah remarked, 'You speak English awfully well.'

'Thank you, Bibi. I was schooled on Charles Dickens, Sir Walter Scott and Evelyn Waugh.'

'Listen, Mr Zafar.'

'Just Zafar, Bibi.'

'Then it'll have to be Farah, not Bibi.'

'People here will consider that familiar,' Zafar pointed out.

'Never mind. A thought has come to mind ... but first tell me, how good are you at a computer?'

'I use it all the time. Most office communication is done on computer.'

'In that case, will you help me with my laptop? My brother Adnan brought me a deluxe unit. I'm not very good at it.'

Zafar was unsure how to respond to this unexpected request.

'Why ... yes ... I can help ... but I feel you should get Kunwar sahib's approval first,' he said finally.

'Yes, of course. And when I do, you won't let me down?'

'No, Bibi. Then it'll be my duty to assist you.'

'You'll be helping me, not serving my father. So a one–to–one approach is preferred, not obsequiousness,' she said tartly as she left the room.

The remark struck him like a slap. He returned to his room wondering why it mattered what she thought of him.

Later that day, Kunwar called Zafar on the phone.

'My daughter tells me that she has spoken to you about software training,' he said.

'Yes, sir,' Zafar replied, surprised at how quickly she had acted.

'I think it's a good idea. You teach her then ... in your spare time. I've told her to call and check when you're free.'

The phone rang as soon as he had finished talking to Kunwar. It was Farah enquiring when they could start computer practice.

For the first few lessons, Zafar used the desktop computer in his office. It was a better training unit than Farah's smaller laptop. Burhan and Abid looked on in amazement until Munshi warned them off.

The training sessions required Zafar and Farah to sit side by side facing the computer screen. Her hands rested on the keyboard while he explained what the signs and symbols meant. Occasionally he reached across her arms to press a key to demonstrate its purpose. Fingers brushed hands inadvertently. At times when she turned towards him for guidance, she would catch him hastily avert his gaze from her face. The fragrance of her hair mingled with his aftershave, creating a heady air of closeness.

When Farah had become reasonably proficient at computing, Zafar switched the practice sessions to the laptop and placed it in Kunwar's office – to avoid peering eyes. He would set her computing tasks and retire to his room, returning periodically to check her progress. Sometimes she performed well. At other times she was unresponsive, preferring to chat. The conversation usually centred on Zafar. She seemed set on 'discovering' him, from life in Khanpur to his presence in Kunwar's home.

Zafar found it difficult to avoid her questions, or resist her efforts to establish a rapport. It was an entirely new experience for him, alien to everything he had known so far in life. He could never have imagined something like this happening to him. He was fascinated by Farah, yet sensed the transience of it all. He felt that if the moment was not grasped now, it might never come his way again. The interest, the ecstasy, the bewilderment were real enough but the social divide between them was daunting.

As for Farah, she found interacting with Zafar a welcome distraction from the situation she found herself in after her engagement to Javed. The uneasiness she had felt after Adnan's return did not cease even after she had accepted Javed's proposal. Her assumption that the marriage might work and would at least help get her away from the family did not lessen the gloom. It diffused gradually as she progressed at computing under Zafar's tutelage.

She found him straightforward and was particularly taken by his beautiful hands, which moved like gazelles on the keyboard. He was unlike the privileged young men she knew. As their rapport developed, she paid no heed to where it may lead. She even spoke about him to her fiancée.

When they worked together, she was not immune to Zafar's understated charm, but it was not until she spotted him rowing a boat on Rawal Lake, where she had gone on a picnic with friends, that she really woke up to his presence.

The glittering water reflected patches of the sun like golden coins on a glass surface, dissolving into molten whorls at the touch of an oar. There was a sharp intake of breath when she observed the solitary oarsman, silhouetted against a watery iridescence, rowing towards a distant destination ... a sight that became etched in her memory.

For the next few days she stayed in her room trying to adjust to new realities. Zafar missed her but was not in a position to make enquiries. On the fourth day she went to the office, steeling herself to cope with life outside the bedroom. Zafar noticed something was amiss. She was withdrawn, avoided his eyes and responded perfunctorily to his remarks.

When they sat facing the laptop screen, she trembled, her hands shaking violently. Zafar, alarmed, reached out instinctively to steady her. As their fingers touched, she clutched his hands and broke into tears. Sobbing, she rested her forehead on their linked hands. Gradually removing his right arm, Zafar placed it round her shoulders.

'Farah Bibi, please ... please don't ... what's the matter ... why are you upset? Is there anything I can do?'

He remained attentive, waiting for her to quieten. After a while, Farah sat up, dabbing her eyes with tissues. It pained him to see her in distress.

'I'm sorry,' she said, 'this should not have happened.'

He brought her a glass of water.

'Let me know if I can help ... anyhow ... anyway...'

'Don't you know what's happened?' she asked on an impulse.

'Happened ... where?'

'Between us,' she said flatly, raising her eyes to him.

He stood still, finding it hard to grasp what she was trying to say.

'Bibi,' he said after a long pause, 'are you saying ... am I to take it that you...?'

'Yes,' she said, coming towards him, 'yes ... me too.'

A sixth sense alerted him to hold back.

'Wait, Bibi,' he said, forwarding a chair, 'let's sit down and talk about this a bit.'

'What,' she said impatiently, 'don't you care ... have you no feeling for me?'

Overcome momentarily, he drew her to himself, holding her hard and fast. She felt his sinewy closeness and gave way to a sense of belonging.

'Care?' he said, kissing her forehead repeatedly. 'I've loved you from the first day when you taunted me...'

She laughed at that.

'I don't know how I've survived so long ... being so close yet unable to touch you,' he went on.

Then, just as swiftly as it had arisen, the joy subsided as the image of his father flashed before him. What an improbable situation he faced: *Kunwar's daughter and a*

*nobody from Khanpur in preference to the governor's son!
What a scandal that would cause. Where could he take
her? How could he shelter her? How would they overcome
the awesome odds?*

His arms went slack, releasing her. She looked up
wondering, about to speak, but he placed a finger on
her lips and said, 'Don't, Bibi, don't say any more. I'm
sorry. I had no right to be so familiar. Forgive me. I don't
want to ruin your life.'

'What are you saying?' she asked, startled by the turn
of events.

'Just that ... that you and I together ... it's
unthinkable ... you belong to a different world ... I'm
too far beneath. There's nothing I can give you to justify
taking you away from all this.'

'But I love you,' she wailed, reaching out to him.

'Bibi, Bibi, it's not enough ... I love you too ... but
how can I take on Kunwar sahib and the world when
I've nothing to offer ... no home ... no livelihood ... no
future but the bits and pieces thrown my way?' he said,
holding her off.

'I have the guts to walk out of my home with you.
What about you?' she asked, crying unrestrainedly.

'Privileged people can afford taking risks. Underdogs
have to struggle for survival.'

'You're wrong,' she said, as she fled, 'wrong ...
wrong ... wrong.'

❦

'Mr Rafiq,' Justice Bilgrami said, 'your application seeking exclusion of Justice Suleiman from the bench on the grounds of bias, is not maintainable.'

'Yes, Your Honour,' Adnan murmured, sitting down.

'You should never have moved that application,' Naqvi admonished Adnan in undertones, 'now they'll have a grouse against us.'

'But Naqvi sahib, our client's stepbrother is Justice Suleiman's ex-son-in-law ... surely these are grounds for a judge to stand down.'

'Ex-son-in-law is an ex-son-in-law, and a stepbrother, a stepbrother. Suleiman has already declared he has nothing to do with him.'

'That's grounds enough. He may harbour a resentment for that reason alone.'

'Judges stand down on substantial grounds, not presumptions.'

'The rules of national justice operate on a presumptive plane.'

'Don't bandy words with me about legal propriety.'

A word from the bench calling for resumption of the hearing silenced them. Naqvi got up to continue the presentation, consigning a dejected Adnan to a back-seat.

The week was going badly for Adnan. Only the previous

day, he had been confounded by jottings of the Attorney General – written before his appointment as Attorney General – on one of the briefs Adnan was studying. They were cross-references to an earlier case handled by the firm. The charges in both cases were similar – the facts matched. In one, the firm had represented the defendant, and in the other, the state. Adnan was struck by the ease with which the Attorney General built up his rationale in the latter case by demolishing the legal premises he had set up in the former case. A handwritten note underscored the irony. It referred to the opposing counsel's arguments in the earlier matter with a view to 'scanning them for sound reasoning which we could use to build up our presentation in the latter case'.

There were more surprises when the Attorney General attended a meeting of the partners and associates at the office. He mentioned that three cases charging high-ranking officials with anti-state activities, being defended by the firm, would end in favour of the firm – they were going to be dismissed. He had succeeded by applying 'official' pressure to convince the prosecution lawyers to withhold incriminating evidence from the bench. He also instructed Naqvi to put up a weak defence in two other cases being handled by the firm, in which powerful interests wanted convictions.

Noticing the look of disbelief on Adnan's face, he said, 'It's often a trade-off, you know. Political interests must be taken into account and results fixed before trial. Your father will explain such matters better than I can.'

These matters were on Adnan's mind when he left the court during the mid-morning recess. He strolled towards the Bar room hoping to catch up with like-minded colleagues over a cup of coffee. On the way, he was drawn aside by an assistant from the Court Registrar's office who placed a slip of paper hastily in his hand. 'Give this to your office head clerk,' he said, before retiring stealthily down a corridor.

The slip bore a reference number, which Adnan recognized as one of his firm's cases, and against it a handwritten date, which fell within the next two weeks.

A colleague in the Bar room explained that the date represented the next 'out of turn' fixture for the hearing of the case wangled by the Registrar's underlings.

'They do this for most law firms, for a fee, of course. Some are on regular payrolls,' he added.

'It's disgusting,' Adnan remarked.

'It's like that from top to bottom,' he said. 'The entire system has been subverted.'

'Is there no way out?' Adnan asked.

'The superior judges try to do the right thing, but poor things, they're reliant on tainted functionaries to carry out their directives. It's a wonder they don't give up in frustration.'

'And you,' Adnan ventured, 'you and others like us, how has this affected our kind?'

His colleague got up to return to court. He stopped at the door, glanced back at Adnan, then said, sotto voce, 'Some are fully compromised; some partly so. There's no way round it. If you want to work in this environment, you'll be tainted sooner or later.'

Adnan looked around the Bar room, sizing up the occupants – groups of old-timers, careworn and rumpled, mostly locally qualified advocates who represented the decay in the system. There were also eminent seniors, impeccably attired in black coats who peeped into the Bar room but never stayed to mingle. They included those who had risen from local ranks and made a quantum leap into a charmed circle, and others who had moved into it laterally from the English Inns of Court to claim the best briefs, the best clients, sinecure status and proximity to the power structure. There were the politically minded lawyers, a motley gathering drawn from all ranks, who supported causes, civil society and social diversity. Then there were savvy new entrants like himself: young men and women from moneyed and middle classes who had graduated from foreign universities and secured their legal colours from British and American law schools.

How many of them, he wondered, *will succumb to the system? How many will strive for the revival of the civil order that existed before the culture of corruption took over? Who will struggle for imposition of a rule of law? And what of me? To which category do I belong?*

❦

There was a flurry of activity in Kunwar's household in preparation for Farah's wedding. Shabana was in her elements dealing with jewellers, dressmakers, beauticians and caterers when not shopping for Farah's dowry from leading stores in London, Rome, New York and elsewhere.

Tariq was responsible for organizing the five functions considered de rigeur for well-to-do parents of brides. He auditioned artistes and pop groups, directed dance sequences that were to be performed by the bride's friends, and instructed event managers on the need for a different setting for each function, ranging from a bacchanal to Arabian Nights.

'For flowers,' he boasted, 'we'll fly in loads of black tulips, blue gardenias, leopard lilies and every goddamn rare bloom in season wherever.'

Kunwar was kept busy with lists of invitees, accommodation for visiting guests, visas for overseas invitees, and running through cheque books to keep up with payments. His office staff worked into the night.

Two persons in the house were scarcely touched by the turmoil. Adnan was oblivious to what went on around him as he walked out and into the house on his way to and from work. Farah kept to her room. She tolerated interruptions only when Shabana sought her for measurements and fittings.

❧

A night before the marriage, Adnan sat working late in the law firm library. Naqvi walked in and placed a file folder before him.

'This brief relates to a minister, who has denied the charges against him. The AG has asked us to prepare a defence as the PM wants him exonerated. Study the papers please and prepare a defence statement. I'll review your draft when completed.'

Adnan looked at the file and could not resist remarking, 'Are we like royal cobblers, here to take the PM's orders to make the shoe fit even if it requires chopping off the big toe?'

'Adnan, I keep telling you to change your attitude. This posturing has been noticed by judges and seniors. It will hamper your progress. You know well that in our legal system an accused person is innocent until proven guilty, and every accused person – even a known serial killer – is entitled to a defence at his trial.'

'Yes sir, yes sir … three bags full, sir.'

Naqvi walked away shaking his head.

As Adnan perused the papers, he felt a black rage

rising within. The implicated minister held the Hajj and religious affairs portfolio. He was accused of levying illegal surcharges on pilgrims' travel papers processed by his department. He was also accused of arranging boarding and lodging in Mecca and Medina of a lesser standard than what the pilgrims had paid for. He and other officials from his department faced charges of extortion, illegal enrichment, fraud, and related offences against the state. Adnan's review of the file enclosures turned up enough grounds for clear-cut charges against the minister and the department secretary, who happened to be a close friend of Kunwar. He found little in the file for a plausible defence. A pilgrim's protest, recorded in the enquiry report, claiming that he had been compelled to commit the sin of bribery with his life savings in order to perform Hajj, brought a rush of tears to Adnan's eyes. He pushed aside the file and strode out of the library without switching off the lights.

When he reached home, he had to manoeuvre his car between parked Mercedes-Benzes, Rolls Royces, Jaguars, reversing drivers and flashing headlights. He was repelled by the spectacle of the ongoing festivities. The house was ablaze with spotlights, mobile laser beams and strands of multicoloured bulbs. A designer version of Haroon-ul-Rashid's court – with dancing girls, drum beaters and Nubian slaves – had been erected on the lawn. A cacophony of rock music, booming drums and Bollywood film songs assailed him. He fought his way indoors through prancing performers, flower throwers, merrymakers including the high and mighty in the land – milling around the obligatory bar serving all kinds of liquor.

It was mehendi night when the bride, attired in plain saffron-coloured clothes, sans make up, hairdo or embellishments, has floral patterns traced with henna on her palms by female friends and relatives of the groom.

Adnan came in and saw Farah, pale, removed, eyes downcast, seated on a dais like a temple figurine. She was surrounded by energetic dancers, flash-lit cameras, audio-visual recorders and onlookers through whom waiters bearing food and drink wended their way. Tariq, in a saffron-coloured designer outfit was everywhere, a veritable master of ceremonies. Both Kunwar and Shabana were noticeable in saffron wear. He in a brocade mandarin coat, and she in a shimmering gown and oversized diamonds. Somehow, Adnan managed to get to Farah and whisper, 'I'm sorry … not been very supportive lately. But I've had important things to sort out … for peace of mind … Love you,' and was gone.

❁

In the early hours of the morning, Adnan came down looking for his family. He found Kunwar, Shabana and

Tariq seated in the alcove, feet up, nibbling leftovers from dinner. All around, workers were busy clearing up remnants and arranging the premises for the next function.

'Where you've been?' Shabana enquired. 'Why you not attending the mehendi, or wearing the Deepak Perwani outfit I order for you?'

'It's not my kind of thing ... besides I didn't want to.'

'What's the matter, son?'

'I'm sick.'

'Sick?' she came towards him, attempting to feel his forehead. 'That's why you're missing all functions? People asked about you. Why you don't tell me before about sickness. Many doctors came to mehendi.'

He moved away uncertainly, and then turned to face them. 'I'm going away,' he said.

'Going where?' Kunwar asked, alarmed.

'Away from all of you ... away from this house ... away from the country ... before I sink deeper in the rot.'

'You've gone mad,' Tariq said, 'you're talking nonsense.'

'Adnan ... my baby,' Shabana sobbed.

'Stop mama, stop whining. I can't stand your tears.'

'Adnan,' Kunwar said sternly, 'take a hold of yourself ... Tariq's right. You're talking nonsense. Explain yourself in plain language. What does this mean?'

'That I've had it up to here,' Adnan said, raising his hand to his chin. 'I can't take the dishonesty ... corruption rampant everywhere ... a credo of self interest above all ... everyone out to do the country in, looting national coffers ... deceiving the public ... defrauding the poor. I won't stay to see everything going to the dogs,' Adnan spat out, breathing in spurts, eyes blazing, beads of perspiration breaking on his forehead.

They were stunned by his outburst. Shabana's sobs punctuated the silence. Recollecting himself, Kunwar came up to Adnan and asked, 'What has all this got to do with your practice ... your career?'

'I see the law being broken every day. Judges' orders ignored, terrible crimes committed unchecked by citizens against citizens ... abduction, rape, murder ... of men, women, children ... white-collar criminals patronized by top people ... security agencies in cahoots with militants ... and we are ordered by big guns to protect them in the courts of law. This is not serving the ends of justice ... it's pandering to mafias, powerbrokers and terrorists bent on ramming their form of religion down our throats ... I want no part of it.'

'You can still have an honourable practice like many others by keeping clear of these things,' Kunwar reasoned.

'How, Papa? Tell me how – like you've done?'

The barb was too palpable to be overlooked. Shabana

shifted uneasily. Kunwar straightened up and took the bait head on.

'Since you've come,' he said, looking Adnan in the eye, 'you've questioned my integrity. I've ignored your impertinence, assuming that your westernized mindset of right and wrong would ultimately get reconciled to local realities, but you persist in your prejudices. So what is it about me that you find objectionable?'

'It's not just you, Papa. It's everyone, your friends, your colleagues, your superiors, your subordinates, the whole stinking lot ... crooks glossed over by a veneer of respectability ... sheer hypocrisy.'

Shabana's sobbing was audible.

'Stop rambling, Bhaijan,' Tariq said, 'and have some concern for Mama's feelings.'

'Oh, she may well weep,' Adnan said, 'you should hear the tales about the loans she has had written off by banks, or the number of designer handbags she purchased on her last trip to London. They say Imelda Marcos was not a patch on her...'

Shabana gasped.

'Shut your mouth,' Tariq yelled, rising to strike his brother.

'Go to hell,' Adnan shouted back.

Tariq lunged at him, but was stopped from landing a blow by Kunwar. He struggled to hold on to Tariq, then said to Adnan, 'Before you pass judgment on us, Mr

Clean, cast your mind to the thousands of dollars it cost to make you a JD. Was that affordable on my salary? Where do you think the money came from?'

There was a pause.

'I'm not passing judgment,' Adnan said, 'only holding up a mirror. Perhaps I'm culpable too, but I was unaware of the true source of my educational expenses, so I couldn't have made any choices then. But now I can, and I choose to go away.'

'Coward,' Tariq snarled, 'why don't you stay and fight the rot?'

'Can't … on my own.'

'Where'll you go? What'll you do?' Shabana asked.

'I have a US work visa, and I have a law degree after all … even if it is somewhat tainted.'

※

On the day of the wedding, Farah awakened Adnan at midday.

'All well?' he asked, stretching and yawning.

'I heard about your showdown with the parents.'

'Good, so now you know.'

'I want to go with you.'

'What?' Adnan exclaimed, sitting up.

'You've taken a decision to leave, and so have I.'

'But what about your marriage this evening?'

'I don't want to get married.'

'Why did you agree?'

'It seemed right to do so at the time.'

'And not now?'

'Now, I have a choice.'

'You're wrong. You had the same choice at that time. Saying "yes" or "no" was up to you. My going away may give you a future opportunity for joining me when I've settled down, but doesn't become an option for you to leave home at this time, on my account.'

'I'm not leaving on your account, silly, but for myself.'

'Then call the parents in and say you want out. You still have to face this evening. It's not like I'm leaving this instant. I'll have to submit my resignation, hand over briefs, settle accounts and finalize travel plans before I can leave. Where do you propose to hide till then?'

❧

Zafar was preparing to go rowing on the afternoon of the wedding. Kunwar had given his office staff the day off. While Munshi and the rest intended to attend the wedding, Zafar preferred to stay away. His plans were disrupted by a hasty call from Munshi summoning him to the office on urgent business. He got to the office in the early afternoon and found Munshi in a terrible state.

'What's the matter?' Zafar asked.

'Burhan died this morning of a heart attack.'

'That's very sad. Does Kunwar sahib know?'

'He's fast asleep. Anyway I'm afraid to tell him before finishing a task he wanted Burhan and me to complete last night. I got delayed doing so because Burhan didn't show up. I thought we could do it today, but now he's gone and the job's not done.'

'Why not just tell Kunwar sahib?'

'No, no, no ... I can't do that. Some transactions have to be completed by certain deadlines. That's why I want your help. If they are not done by this evening, he'll kill me.'

'How can I help?'

'Well, you know how to operate a computer and send emails.'

'That's all?'

'You have to access certain password-protected websites...' Munshi said, then paused before continuing, 'mind you, don't mention any of this to Kunwar sahib.'

Zafar was puzzled. Seeing his look of concern, Munshi explained, 'Kunwar sahib confided these matters to Burhan and me. You're not supposed to know about them.'

'Then don't tell me.'

'It's necessary for getting the job done.'

'Why can't it be done later?'

'Because Kunwar sahib will be penalized by persons above him if certain payments are not made today.'

Zafar reluctantly agreed to help. Munshi bolted the office doors, unlocked a drawer in Burhan's desk, drew out a notebook with a patterned cover, pored over its contents, turning pages back and forth, looking for certain information. When he found it, he jumped with excitement.

'Here it is ... here ... here,' he said, thrusting the book under Zafar's nose.

Zafar saw a combination of letters, numbers and symbols suggesting a website.

'Now punch them in and access the site,' Munshi directed.

Zafar turned on the computer and did as asked. He had to follow many complex instructions before a secured site appeared. The image on the screen was a replica of the notebook cover.

Munshi studied the notebook, then instructed Zafar to open page 3 on the screen. Page 3 contained a list of letter combinations which Zafar recognized as ledger reference identifications. Page 4 contained a list of colours: 'red', 'blue', 'green' and other shades. Page 5 contained names and email addresses of banks located abroad.

Munshi pulled out a handwritten note from his briefcase, studied it, then told Zafar to access some of the banks listed and instruct them to transfer funds in amounts he mentioned from the letter combinations specified by him, to 'red', or 'blue', or 'green' as he directed. Zafar did so. He typed instructions for several transfers and pressed the 'send' key for each transaction. He was dismayed when the computer aborted the dispatches owing to improper entry of letter combinations. Munshi panicked, when told of the failure.

'Do something,' he said, 'they must go … you know how the damn thing works.'

A telephone rang persistently in Kunwar's office. Munshi went off, to stall the caller. While he was gone, Zafar made three more attempts – unsuccessfully – to make the transfers. After the third try, a message on screen directed the user to check correct entries on page 1. When Zafar opened the page, the letter combinations sprang up, each followed by a highlighted index number, title of a government project, its contract value, particulars of the official signatory, identification of the project executor and reserved commission figures.

Zafar automatically substituted the index numbers for the letter combinations he had entered earlier, and succeeded finally in dispatching the data. When he had finished, he recalled – with a pounding heart – that the entries on page 1 related to certain recognizable government projects. Anxious to discover the true nature of what he had done, he accessed page 2. On it, he was appalled to see that the colours represented various government functionaries, their foreign bank account numbers and addresses. Hearing Munshi's step, he reverted hastily to the book cover image.

Munshi asked, 'Is it done?'

Zafar nodded. As the significance of the transaction dawned on him, Zafar felt a stabbing pain in the pit of his stomach.

'It was Kunwar sahib, chasing me to check whether the transfers had been completed,' Munshi said, humming a tune and replacing the notebook.

'I told him they were ... for which I must thank you. I didn't inform him of Burhan's death; otherwise he might have asked awkward questions, forcing me to lie. Anyway it's bad luck to talk of death at a wedding. Tomorrow I'll tell him. The show will be over and he'll be relieved.'

Zafar did not hear him; he was in the washroom throwing up.

When he returned to his rented premises that evening, Zafar wrote two letters. One, a letter of resignation to Kunwar, the second, an enquiry to the organization working for poverty alleviation, on jobs available.

❀

As a bride, Farah looked less than radiant. Something was amiss. She seemed in a trance. Her movements were stiff and doll-like. She sat for hours, in bridal finery and glittering jewellery on a flower-strewn dais in her bedroom, waiting. Her moment would come when the nikah witnesses came to ask if she consented to the marriage. Adnan looked in on her and wondered what she had decided, and why she had left it to the last minute. She did not look at him. Shabana sensed her daughter's unease, but did not express concern, fearing unwelcome responses. She waited by Farah's side along with Farah's close friends.

In the living room downstairs, all eyes were on the maulana who sat beside the gilded groom. He was busy making handwritten entries in the *nikahnama* which represented the marriage certificate. When that was over, he dispatched the marriage witnesses to obtain the bride's consent.

People downstairs sat in anticipation for their return. Adnan watched from above as the witnesses wound their way up the circular staircase, pass him by and approach Farah's room. Voices in the room were lowered when they appeared at the door. The leader paused, then declared the terms of the proposal in a prescribed form. Finally, he asked Farah in ringing tones, 'Do you consent to this marriage?'

'Farah,' Shabana said after a pause, 'they're waiting for your response to marrying Javed … say "yes".'

There was no response. Farah sat still, looking down, motionless. Everyone held their breath. Again, Shabana reminded her about the witnesses and urged her with mounting anxiety to say 'yes'.

Farah stirred but said nothing. Despairing, Shabana moved as close as possible to Farah and whispered fiercely in her ear, 'Say "yes", Farah, or you'll disgrace us. If you don't want to speak, just nod your head. If you refuse this match,' she threatened, 'I'll damn you with curses … curses and hellfire.'

Farah gasped and looked up at the mother, moving her chin involuntarily. Seizing on Farah's reactions, Shabana leapt up screaming, 'She said "yes" … "yes" … "yes" … and even nodded her head.'

There was some confusion. People were not sure about what they had heard or seen. Shabana moved swiftly towards the witnesses to confirm Farah's consent. They went downstairs armed with Farah's 'response'.

The maulana solemnized the marriage, concluding with a moving passage from the Quran. Adnan, who watched from above, shook his head in disbelief. 'So that's that,' he muttered.

Farah finally came out of the trance and said 'No', in a low voice. Then 'no' louder, and louder, and louder still, but no one heard her. She was alone in the bedroom. The others had gone downstairs for the finale.

Through the Lattice

'Chumpa ... Chumpa,' a voice called and for a moment she became the flower again.

A sparrow joined her in the covered bus stand. It reminded her of the birds fluttering through the lattices of the veranda at the 'big house' where she had spent much of her childhood.

Her earliest memories were of bouncy rides in a sling on her mother's back when she left home at dawn for the 'big house'. She recalled using the sandalwood crib in the veranda while her mother dusted and cleaned, going up and down the stairs. The world outside became hers in snatches through the crisscrossed openings. Sunlight entered in diamond-shaped spots that stretched and lengthened across the tiled floor. Chumpa crawled – and later, toddled – wherever she wanted, cosseted by family and staff alike, safe within the lattices, safe in the 'big house' that stood between the peasant settlement and the village.

At five, she was taken aback one day to find herself in her aunt's cottage without her mother. She did not know at the time that she would never see her mother again. Gradually, she was told that her parents had been run over by a truck swerving to avoid a bullock cart.

She cried for two days, refused to eat, calling out for her mother and repeating the names of the people at the 'big house'. That changed somewhat when a limousine drove up to her aunt's yard bringing the Begum from the 'big house'.

'My little bud,' the Begum said, hugging her. 'Khadija Bibi,' she said, addressing Chumpa's aunt, who was overcome by the unexpected visit, 'I wonder whether you'll consider leaving Chumpa with me when you're busy at the village school.'

'Begum Sahiba,' the aunt said, eyes brimming with tears, 'that's very kind of you ... but Allah has finally taken pity on me and sent me my brother's *nishani*. He's given me my own flesh and blood after all these years. How can I let her go?'

Chumpa sensed that they were talking about her. Feeling insecure, she crept close to the Begum and held tightly on to her.

'Silly,' the Begum said, 'I'm not asking you to give up Chumpa. Just let her be with me while you're doing your chores.'

The aunt did not reply, busy as she was serving tea. The Begum talked about improvement schemes she proposed for the settlement and her plans for Chumpa.

'They're all good things ... what you want to do for us,' the aunt said finally. 'I'm ready to bring her to you not because of them. It's because of the way she clings to you. She seems to need you.'

After the Begum left, she told her husband, 'It's Allah's will, so it has to be good.'

❀

How the children jumped with joy at having me back, Chumpa recalled gleefully at the bus stand. *Was it really fourteen years ago?*

'Mother,' said the girls, one after another, to the Begum, 'we'd like Chumpa with us when the ustaad from the school comes.'

'Of course, but bear in mind, she has never studied before ... so it'll take time to get her used to lessons.'

The boys joined in, demanding that they be allowed to play 'seven tiles' with the peasant girl.

'Begum Sahib,' the cook – the oldest retainer at the 'big house' – said, 'you did well to bring Chumpa *bitya* back. The place has come alive.'

It had been a homecoming of sorts, Chumpa remembered. Her roots were in her aunt's cottage but the 'big house' represented her world. If she was treated like family there, she was equally at home with the peasants. As a child, she moved between the two with the ease of a bird flying between branches.

There were moments, of course, that had been disquieting.

'What's she doing here?' Jagirdar Malik Aslam had asked his wife, the Begum, when he saw Chumpa one afternoon.

Chumpa recalled stopping in her tracks.

'She spends the day here while her aunt goes to work at the school house.'

'Since when?'

'For a while.'

'Why?' He frowned as he spoke.

'She belongs here,' the Begum replied.

'I don't understand.'

'Listen, her mother came with me when I married you.'

'Yes, yes, she was your maid. So?'

'She was more – a childhood friend – my father told you.'

'Big deal! I'd say you did well by her. You asked me to find a husband for her among our local men. I did. He was one of my favourites, the estate irrigation foreman. You paired them off and also made me give them a homestead … with … cultivable land, nearby. But why this?'

'Yes, but she died while in our service. People now expect us to support her child – who's an orphan – so I'm keeping her here and training her to manage the house and assist me in the tedious functions expected of jagirdarnis.'

'But these things are usually handled by the male staff.'

'Darling, please stop viewing the world through feudal lenses. Look at her. She's pretty, gifted and has a strong personality.'

Chumpa had felt her cheeks burning.

'She'll handle anything … given a chance. Don't forget, you promised my father, we would continue living like your liberal ancestors in the Raj … and … and … give a wide berth to the sick segregated lifestyle being foisted on us.'

The Begum laughed softly.

'Why else do you think, I agreed to marry you?'

Malik Aslam thoughtfully stroked his moustache. A smile lit his handsome face. He patted Chumpa on the head.

'All right, have it your way, but try not to cross too many lines. You're taking on peoples' lives here.'

❀

Chumpa recalled falling in readily with the Begum's plans. She was a quick learner, an apt pupil, skilled at computing, capable at practical tasks. By the age of eighteen, she was performing her duties with breezy confidence.

When she stepped in for the day, the house seemed to awaken. She allotted tasks to daily-wage workers and outdoor labour, checked the laundry, oversaw the cleaning and renovation of the premises and replenished household provisions. She also helped in the kitchen and kept the girls company.

Her name resounded everywhere. Even the six caged South American parakeets in their niches echoed, 'Chumpa,' 'Chumpa,' as she trod the corridors, braids swinging. At dusk, she gave a report to the Begum, took instructions for the next day and left for her aunt's. When she went, a hush descended.

The Begum basked in Chumpa's success.

'She's not just a housekeeper,' she insisted, urging Chumpa to come and live with them.

Though drawn to the idea, Chumpa resisted the move. Living at the 'big house' would prove complicated. It threatened to be stifling, and – her aunt had cautioned – likely to bring her face to face with feudal prejudices. Her relatively smooth relationship with the Begum – and hard-won status – risked being compromised.

With hindsight, the happiness of the time seemed magical but unreal.

❀

As a flock of sheep surrounded the bus stand, Chumpa covered herself with a chadar to avoid being recognized.

It was that winter – years later, she recalled, *when the Begum's elder son turned twenty-one – that a change came about.*

'Hurry up, Chumpa, pile my hair up like yours. I want to look stylish. Our brothers will be here soon,' said the Begum's elder daughter.

'Bibijan, my braids aren't pinned up for style. With my kind of work it's just easier that way.'

'Chumpa,' the younger daughter said, 'mother wants to know if everything's in order.'

'Yes, yes, Bibigul. We've been celebrating your brothers' homecoming every year, since they went to university. So why the fuss?'

'Except this time we'll have their college mates as guests.'

'Don't worry, all will be well.'

'Come on girls,' the Begum called, passing by, 'I hear a car in the driveway.'

Chumpa watched the young men getting out of the cars and making their way into the house. There were ten in all, including the Begum's sons. She tried to identify the foreigners, hoping the arrangements for them would prove suitable. Bedrooms had been allotted. Two English guests – one related to British royalty – were to share a single bedroom suite on the upper floor. A Sheikh from Abu Dhabi, a well-heeled Indian and a Taiwanese were given separate bedrooms. Three visitors 'from home' would be sharing a two-bedroom suite with a lounge for the 'men only' sessions they planned to hold on the ground floor.

The young men were greeted by their hosts. The Begum, graceful in a sari and a jamavar shawl, had been effusive. Malik Aslam, in a black achkan sporting regimental colours and turban topped with a fan-shaped crest, was a little stiff.

The blonde Englishmen and the smiling Taiwanese chatted easily with the two awestruck girls. The Indian listened politely to the Begum's account of her last trip to India. The two Pakistanis conversed in Urdu while the third stood aside with the Arab, sipping white wine, his flashing black eyes taking in the setting, Malik Aslam's polo trophies and the girls. When he glanced quizzically at Chumpa, she turned uneasily away.

Later she felt awkward when conducting the guests to their rooms. There was a sense of being watched, of furtive glances being exchanged and innuendo being traded. She felt exposed, vulnerable.

Her dealings with men had been somewhat different. As the Begum's protégé in the 'big house', she had a privileged status, exempt from unwanted male attention. She had learnt all she could from her aunt about how to deal with the problem of the village male's stare. But foreigners and the rich were a different matter.

Chumpa recalled darting here and there, somewhat dazed, trying to keep pace with the various events planned. December was a festive season in the 'big house'. She was aware that this would be a more magical December than any she had seen before – since Malik Aslam desired that the guests be royally entertained. Besides Christmas and New Year celebrations – and his elder son's twenty-first birthday – there were to be archaeological outings, shikar, a mujra evening, a picnic, a riverside barbecue and, of course, partying nonstop.

The larder and refrigerated storages were glutted with all kinds of food. Alcohol flowed. Additional service staff, cars and gunmen were hired and party paraphernalia assembled. Two popular rock groups were booked and people of repute in the city invited to dinner and dance parties at the 'big house'.

Chumpa was relieved that her workload gave her little time to mingle with the visitors. The children of the household were like family, but she found that the guests were a different sort. So she kept her distance from them. But she could not help running into them from time to time, at large in the house, playing riotous games in the garden, at bridge or billiards, cracking smutty jokes while watching video films and then vanishing all at once in a flash of cars – languid, graceful and, yes, even amiable.

As the days passed, the strangeness seemed to wear off, out of necessity initially – she found herself stitching on missing buttons, producing aspirin for headaches, helping tie turbans for the mujra. Later, the contrived distance was dispensed with by choice. After a halting start, Chumpa was able to chat with the foreign guests in English. Communication aroused a sense of closeness.

She was not a little surprised to discover how well she eventually got on with the guests – except for the dark-eyed Nawab Khusro Nawaz Jung, who seemed to size her up when he first came. He was clearly a flirt. She saw him chatting up Bibijan, in the garden and dogging her throughout the day. The next day she was ignored while he gave Bibigul the chase. At the dances, both sisters were overlooked. Instead, he decided to charm some of the female guests. Then he rediscovered Bibijan and more or less stayed the course. So it seemed quite in the order of things for Bibijan to seek Chumpa's opinion of Khusro.

'You mean the one you can't take your eyes off, Bibijani?'

'Be serious. Do you like him?'

'Well, he's tall and handsome ... a little snooty perhaps, and a bit too fond of liquor, but he'll do for you, jani ... when he stops chasing other women.'

'How can you say such things? You're a child.'

'I'm old enough to know about your riding with him on the farm, mooning over each other in the billiards room, disappearing in the rose garden. Shall I go on?'

'Chumpa ... he wants to marry me.'

'O God, does the Begum know?'

'Of course. His parents will visit to propose formally, that's ... if ... I agree.'

Chumpa suggested she wait a while.

'Would you do that in my place?' the older girl asked.

'You want a child to answer that?' she asked mockingly. Then more seriously, 'Yes, I would. I'd wait.'

Just then the Begum swept in.

'Well, darling, what've you got to say?' she asked with barely concealed excitement. 'Your father is expected to give a response to Khusro's parents soon.'

'Begum Sahiba,' Chumpa interjected, 'give her time to think. This matter concerns her life.'

'Chumpa,' the Begum said sharply, 'your comments are out of place.'

❈

A gust of cold air swept through the bus stand. Chumpa shivered and drew the chadar closer. It was almost as chilly as the morning after Bibijan's engagement to Nawab Khusro, when Chumpa trudged through soggy fields to the 'big house'. Peasant farmers working in the fields greeted her as she went by.

'Off to the "big house", girlie?' enquired a white-bearded field hand holding up his scythe.

'Yes, Baba, as always,' she replied, inhaling the smell of freshly cut alfalfa, dupatta fluttering in the morning breeze.

'Such a little girl running such a large house. How do you do it?' he asked, wrinkling his brow.

'Allah's help and Begum Sahiba's training.'

'I've watched you pass by for many years, growing out of childhood, wondering what will become of you.'

'Why Baba?' Chumpa said surprised. 'Pray good things come my way.'

'I do. We all do. Allah protect you from the evil eye.'

Cries of 'Chumpa Baji, Chumpa Baji' wafted through the air. Children on their way to school were calling. She waved to them.

After a while, she saw a trail of dust raised by a convoy of vehicles bearing a shikar party from the 'big house'.

'Chumpa, Chumpa,' they yelled, passing her.

The party was smaller than anticipated.

'Nawab Sahib and Mr David ... not with you?' she enquired, noticing the absence of Khusro and an English guest.

'Khusro's doing the traditional thing, packing up and going home after the engagement. David's just being a pain ... says he's against hunting.'

'Tell us, fragrant white blossom,' called one of them, 'what shall we bring back for you? A buck or a bird?'

'All you're good for, you old bore,' responded another, mockingly to the first, 'is a black boar.'

The round of laughter that followed from the vehicles was interrupted by the other Englishman, 'I say a lion, a lion is what we'll bag for Chumpa.'

She smiled, waved, zigzagging gingerly between dung heaps and cud-chewing buffalo to a canal route that led directly to the big house.

The oval-shaped dome and turrets of the 'big house' emerged like spectres in the morning mist. As she approached the driveway, brooding sunlight touched the façade of the whitewashed structure. Inside, it was silent – the banter and play gone with the hunting party.

She attended to the disarray – soiled carpets, chipped ormolu clock, peeling tapestry, askew ancestral portraits. When she had finished, the cook wanted her to prepare spices for the game the hunters would bring back. Instead, she went upstairs.

She was concerned about Bibigul being on her own. Bibijan had been sent to her grandmother's on account of a taboo on betrothed couples staying in the same house before the wedding.

In the corridor, she heard muffled sounds from the guest suite occupied by the two English boys. Perplexed, she went in to check. Startled by a sudden movement in the dressing area of the room, she looked up. It was David. Six feet tall, he stood there naked, glistening in dripping bathwater. Both stared at each other impassively. In a moment, he had run back to the bathroom, while she fled towards the stairs – tripping and landing in Khusro's way, who was passing by the foot of the stairs, bag in hand, on his way to the car waiting to take him home.

Khusro dropped his bag and was instantly at her side, kneeling to help her. She struggled to cover splayed limbs. Within a moment, he had lifted and carried her to his room, placing her on the bed – where she lay wide-eyed and shivering. She could still taste the water he coaxed her to sip. His hands steadied her twitching limbs, easing her. Then in a flash they were at her clothes. She felt the sudden weight of his body, the reek of alcohol on his breath, the stubble searing her face, teeth biting her flesh. Her screams were silenced by dizzying slaps stifled by a cloth, while her arms and legs flailed – enmeshed butterfly. Just as her resistance was about to give way,

he was plucked from her forcibly by David, who dashed
in partly clothed on hearing her scream.

❀

*Did I ever thank my rescuer for covering me with a
blanket ... afterwards,* she wondered.

Chumpa looked up at a flock of birds flying over
the bus stand, to dispel the memory of those dreadful
moments. Her mind wandered back to the discussion
that took place on that fateful day between the Begum
and Malik Aslam when she had lain slumped on the
carpeted floor, listening.

'What're we going to do about this business?' the
Begum had said in a distracted undertone.

'Nothing much at this stage ... unless there are
repercussions,' he replied, inclining his head towards
Chumpa, shoulders braced, hands behind his back.

'I mean the wedding. How do we get out of it?'

'Why get out ... let's go ahead with it as planned.'

'You can't be serious. Not with that ghastly Khusro,
after what he tried to do to this poor child.'

'Well, he didn't succeed, did he?' Malik Aslam said in
a taunting voice.

'For God's sake! Suppose he'd tried to molest our
younger one.'

'How can you even think that,' he snapped.

'But supposing he had?'

Malik Aslam frowned.

'That would be a violation of the code.'

'And what was this?'

'You know well enough what position a servant girl has in her feudal lord's home,' he said.

'That's old-fashioned nonsense,' she said, with a trace of disgust.

'Look,' Malik Aslam said in a firmer tone, 'Khusro's family is top drawer. He's expected to graduate from Cambridge with a starred first. We couldn't do better. The girl's not been damaged. No one other than us – and the three involved – knows what happened. Khusro left, without any fuss so that Bibijan could come home and the English lad has promised to be discreet. So, for me, the matter's closed. As for this ... this creature,' he continued, jerking his head towards Chumpa, 'she'll have to keep her mouth shut. Who'll believe her anyway ... especially if we say she's ... generally amenable?'

Chumpa felt chilled by the words and saw her world coming apart as the Begum's beautiful face seemed to crumple up.

'I've never heard you say such things before,' the Begum said, reaching out in a cajoling manner. 'Surely, you wouldn't do something so awful when it's not even her fault?'

'Just watch,' he said, shaking her off.

'It's not fair ... not right,' the Begum said, 'that fellow

being rewarded with our daughter and this girl having to pay.'

He interrupted. 'For being in the wrong place at the wrong time ... for disturbing the order of our lives.'

She turned to him in disbelief. 'This side of you ... it's something I ... I expect ... all these years ... and I never suspected anything. Your liberal beliefs ... I take, they were a sham.'

'Stop ... just stop,' he said suddenly, seizing her wrist. 'I'll take all necessary steps to preserve order. You know that much about me.'

He let go of her wrist. She staggered back.

'Now get rid of her,' he half-shouted as a thought seemed to strike him. 'Her presence will spoil the marriage and embarrass Khusro. If you don't dispose of her soon, I have ways of doing so.'

'But we brought her up along with our children,' the Begum protested, feeling her wrist.

'Actually,' he said with something like contempt, 'it was stupid of you to try to pass off a wretched thing from the settlement as one of us.'

With that, Malik Aslam strode off banging the door shut. The Begum fell back in a chair sobbing – shoulders hunched, no more the imperious chatelaine, merely a landowner's wife. She looked at Chumpa for a fleeting moment, face wet with tears, then got up from the chair and left.

Abandoned by her champion, cast out, ostracized, Chumpa was quite lost. She recalled her deep sense of betrayal and humiliation. She had even been denied the right to speak for herself. The enormity of the injustice had been unbearable.

She retreated to the settlement, burying herself at her aunt's, refusing to face the world. The presence of her aunt had been comforting. Aware of the speculation in the village, Chumpa had found solace in the stoical silence of the peasants. No one knew what had really happened because Chumpa said nothing and reports from the 'big house' were distorted.

'Bitya, your name can't be uttered at the "big house",' the old cook told Chumpa on a secret visit, 'but that won't keep me from you.'

She looked up gratefully.

'They're worried, bitya,' he continued.

'What about?' she enquired.

'They don't want Khusro Nawab's name linked to your going away.'

'Why not ... that's the truth, isn't it?'

'I overheard Malik Saheb saying it would have a bad political effect.'

'I don't understand.'

'Khusro Nawab's family is losing voter support in its home base to some man, some lawyer.'

'How does that affect the "big house"?'

'Not sure ... but they fear that if this gets out, it'll blacken them. Whatever happens, most people who know you, believe that your dismissal is a cover for some big blunder of the jagirdars.'

'Do they?' she asked, feeling tears pricking her eyes.

'Come on, bitya, whose side do you think the locals will take if the jagirdars try to harm you? Most people, whether village folk or peasants, remember you as the kisaan baby who lived in the latticed veranda and grew up to run the jagirdar's house. They know the truth ... they know ... they know.'

The cook's words helped but her despondency persisted. She took to going out by herself during the evening hours. Venturing into the sunlight one day, she wandered through wheat fields, listlessly trampling blood-red poppies, eventually stopping at her parents' cottage. It looked derelict, abandoned, the surroundings overgrown with creepers and wild plants, the fruit trees untended, the well unused, the pulley silent. On her way back, the ustaad appeared suddenly – walking stick in one hand, Urdu newspaper in the other.

'Caught you finally,' he remarked with a hint of a smile.

She was startled. 'Assalamalaikum, sir,' she said deferentially, covering her head.

'I've been looking for you. Where've you been all this time?'

'At home ... recovering ...getting over a fever,' she said, taking in his solicitous face, starched salwar kameez and eternal waistcoat.

'Now that you've left the "big house", what'll you do?' he asked, looking at her squarely.

'Haven't thought about that,' she said, a little taken aback.

'Well, I could find work for you, but I think it's time you married, settled down.'

'Why ... why are you talking of marriage?' she retorted.

'There doesn't seem to be any other way.'

'I don't understand. Why must I marry, sir?'

There was perplexity and indignation in her voice.

'For your good name. You won't be able to manage without a husband when your aunt and uncle go. A woman needs the protection of a man.'

'Why?' she protested bitterly.

'Because that's the way it is. How it's always been.'

'It needn't be so. You said the new century would bring change.'

She scanned his face hopefully for a moment.

'You need to look around,' he said abruptly, adding, 'what other choices do women like you have? I may have said what I did, but nothing really changes ... you know that.'

There was a pause during which she shifted her

weight uneasily from foot to foot, anxious to leave but not moving for fear of offending him.

'Sir, why are my future plans important to you?' she asked, impatient to get away.

'You were my pupil at the "big house", so I feel responsible,' he said with a catch in his voice. 'My best pupil. You believed, mistakenly, that your future lay in the "big house". I could've told you otherwise.'

'I see ... and now you'd like to help,' she said, somewhat mollified.

'Yes, I would,' he said. 'You're sufficiently educated,' he continued, 'to make an enlightened wife for a decent man. You'll also make a good teacher. After marriage, you can join our teaching staff at the school.' He reflected a while, then said, 'You know, the greengrocer and the muezzin of the village mosque would make good husbands ... I'll arrange a match with the one you prefer.'

She looked up affronted.

'I don't want to marry either.'

'But they're respectable fellows who would raise your social status.'

'So what?' she said indignantly. 'They would be marrying me because of you, sir, and out of pity. Either way, I'd be beholden ... beneath them ... not a good way to start a marriage. Such respectability would be ... would be ... too much of a burden.'

'Well then,' he said, after a pause, 'you'd best settle for someone from your community.'

'What's wrong with that, sir?' she retorted, 'at least we'll be one of a kind … trying to lead a proper life, like my aunt and uncle.'

'Chumpa, I see there's much anger in you … and … I believe … it's justified. You were indeed let down. Many in the village know you're a decent girl. Some want to help. Is there anything I can do?' he said.

A truckload of oranges passed by the bus stand, reminding Chumpa of the citrus grove in which she got married to a kinsman selected by her aunt.

The couple's consent to the marriage was taken and the Quran recited by the village imam, followed by a meal of barbecued lamb, seasoned rice, spiced yogurt and butter milk. There was singing and dancing in the spaces between the orange trees. At sunset, drumbeaters accompanied the couple home, chanting the valedictory bridal song: *Forsaking the hearth of elders, I go today to my lover's vale…*

On reaching a mud-plastered structure standing amidst yellow-flowered mustard fields, the bridegroom – strapping, silent – suddenly slipped away, leaving her, bedecked and shrouded, in the company of staring poultry and livestock. What seemed like hours later, he stumbled in, burping, reeking of bhang and tharra. Blindly, he reached for her. She fought him off. But he proved stronger. He struck her again and again until she lay passive and still. Then he took her with quiet ferocity.

The next morning – *What, was it only two days ago?* Chumpa wondered – she appeared at her aunt's, battered, bleeding in her bridal finery.

'What I would've parted with on my wedding night was snatched from me,' she protested.

'Men are like that,' said her aunt, turning from the stove to tend to Chumpa.

Yes, thought Chumpa, staring at the crushed petals in her hennaed hands, *they are. Whisky fumes transmuting into malted bhang … manicured hands turning into rustic fingers … grappling, grasping … predator thwarted … predator triumphant. Yes, they are … they're … all the same.*

'Even your uncle was jungli when young,' her aunt said, mopping Chumpa's brow with her dupatta.

'But what am I going to do?' wailed Chumpa. 'I can't go back to him … I won't.'

'Be still Chumpa,' her aunt said, stroking her head. 'I said I'd get you a good man. I still believe he's good, no matter what's happened.'

'How can I forget it?'

'Chumpa,' her aunt said after a while, 'there's

something I must tell you. He's never been with a woman before … any woman … you were the first.'

Chumpa stopped crying, nonplussed.

'How … how do you know?'

'Your uncle spied him in the bazaar early this morning, vomiting outside the pharmacy. It didn't take him long to find out why.'

'What did he say?'

'His fear of not managing on the wedding night drove him to ask friends for advice.'

'Friends!' Chumpa remarked shrilly.

'They told him how to do it.'

'What?'

'They plied him with bhang and alcohol to arouse him. They didn't realize he'd turn violent.'

'They aroused the creature who went for me,' Chumpa said with rising anger.

'Hush, child … hush … it's our fault.'

'Whose fault?'

'Ours, us womenfolk. We raise our sons to be men.'

'But not to brutalize. You have married me to a simpleton, who was encouraged by buffoons to hurt me. Has he no mind of his own?'

'He has … he has. You knew that he's a matriculate … supports his parents … has married off his sisters … owns land, a tractor on hire-purchase and farm animals. His kind struggles hard for a home. He wouldn't marry until he'd built his own, away from the parents. That's why you agreed to marry him.'

'So what?'

'He'll soon realize the importance of having a wife at home. Men appreciate such things after everything's in place. See how it is with your uncle and me ... and I never even gave him a child. Instead, we accepted you as our own.'

'But what's there in this mess for me?' Chumpa said, sobbing silently.

The aunt placed baked bread and tea before Chumpa, then reverted to the stove.

'Listen, Chumpa,' she said after a while, 'your marriage didn't happen easily.'

'What do you mean?' Chumpa asked, sitting up.

'Well, you know,' her aunt said, selecting her words carefully, 'the biradari never quite approved of your mother's connection with the "big house". I remember warning your mother – bless her soul – after she married my brother, but the Begum was too strong for her. It's the same in your case.'

Chumpa looked up, incredulous.

'Not many were ready when we sought proposals for you. People think you're good, but not as a daughter-in-law.'

'But I'm educated and can do many things – thank God.'

'Doesn't help. You're half *kisaan*, neither peasant nor princess.'

Chumpa was silenced by the revelations.

'But *he* liked your looks, your education, your standing at the "big house". He said you were special.'

'So what do you want me to do?'

'Go home, Chumpa, and wait for your man. Without a home, a woman's nothing. Remember, it's we who keep the stove lit. Man doesn't do that, yet he'll lay his life down for a home – even if he never admits that he cares.'

'But, Phuppo, the being together turns my stomach.'

'Adjust, like we've all had to. Allah made us for mating with men … for having children.'

'I won't be abused again.'

'He's over that, I'm sure.'

'A woman, even a wife, should be asked if she's wants to take part in such acts.'

'A man's power lies in spreading the seed. Why has Allah allowed them four wives? Women are made for bearing children. Just one seed impregnates. She can carry only one man's child at a time.'

'Is that all sex is for … babies?'

'It also brings husband and wife together. It makes them one.'

'What I went through was nothing like that.'

'No, no, no … your experience was bad. It shouldn't

have been that way. A couple must try to work things out peacefully. When they fit together, it's fine.'

'What if it doesn't happen?'

'Won't happen when a couple is ill-suited.'

'So it's a chance one takes.'

'A choice one makes, as your uncle and I did. Why do you think he didn't marry again even though I was barren?' she asked, winking at Chumpa as she knotted her greying hair.

'You make everything sound ... so ... so normal,' Chumpa said, leaning back.

'Just an old peasant speaking her mind,' she chuckled, a twinkle lighting her eye.

❈

All day long, Chumpa sat at the bus stand reflecting on life. As the evening drew closer, passengers continued getting on and off buses. She did not seem part of the melee of people, vehicles, animal-drawn carts and bicycles – all in constant motion. She tried to visualize life in the cities, where some coaches were headed.

I feel I can survive on my own anywhere, despite the odds ... no one can take away the ustaad's teaching and the Begum's training, she reasoned. *But wait ... what was it aunt said about the significance of a home ...she spoke of the need of a man and a home ... is hers the only course open to me?*

It dawned on her that her aunt had echoed much of what the ustaad had said. While mulling over her options, it came to her with a start that she had a home too – not the aunt's place, not the mud-plastered marital hutment, nor even the 'big house' – but her parents' cottage – somewhat rundown perhaps, but surrounded by fertile land dotted with wild flowers and fruit trees. Perhaps she could fix it and make it habitable – a place for unwinding, for planning one's life – a place of one's own. Chumpa got up to leave the bus stand.

A Touch of Humanity

On her thirty-ninth birthday, Meher Bano found herself in an ambulance accompanying her husband to the hospital. He had collapsed after a coughing fit. She looked at the still body – eyes shut, face ashen, ventilator-mask covering his mouth. Drops from a plastic bag snaked through the intravenous drip into his arm.

She wondered what lay ahead. There was a sense of déjà vu. Much of her life had been spent in a state of anticipation. Never sure what to expect, she had learnt to cope with each new situation as it arose.

She was dimly aware that her circumstances were more or less beyond her control. The eldest of eleven children, she had been cast very early on in the unenviable role of nursemaid to her brothers and sisters, owing largely to her mother's dementia.

Marriage had also proven elusive. If frail, ailing Syed

Nadeem Rizvi had not come calling looking for a good name to wed, Meher, daughter of Moulvi I. Ahmed, may have remained unwed.

That day in the ambulance she felt nothing for Nadeem – not even when, at the hospital, she was told by the doctor on duty that he had died of asphyxiation on the way. It struck her as ironic that death had been caused not by his multiple ailments but by choking on a slice of her birthday cake.

Nadeem had never really been her partner in life. He was primarily concerned with the prospect of siring a male offspring. Attempts towards this end had led to the birth of three daughters and several miscarriages in fifteen years of marriage.

While waiting for the death certificate, Meher caught a glimpse of herself in a wall mirror. The face that stared back was puffy and red veined. The limpid eyes looked haunted. She felt trapped. If there had been some relief during her dismal stay in Nadeem's home, it had come from raising the girls and working for an NGO promoting legal rights of women prisoners.

✳

After the funeral, Meher moved back to her father's home. That was a mistake. She was expected to resume running the house and overseeing her mother. Her presence in the house also provided an excuse for the siblings to leave their children in her care when they were occupied. She was kept on her toes. The NGO was ignored. When the demands of the family became excessive, she decided it was time to leave.

'Where will you go?' Moulvi I. Ahmed asked.

'I'll find a flat in a nice residential area.'

'You and the girls will live there alone?'

'Yes, what of it?'

'It's unheard of … highly improper … People will talk.'

'Abba, those days are gone … even women in villages go about earning a living … As for gossip …'

'You'll still have a problem getting a good flat in a respectable neighbourhood.'

'I know that … don't worry, I've already put word out.'

'That was quick … but have you enough money to pay rent … and run a home?'

'Nadeem's estate brings in something.'

'It was taken over by his brothers though, wasn't it?'

'There's my share … the girls have theirs too.'

'You'll be lucky to get something from them.'

※

Three months later, Meher was reminded of what her father had said. Nadeem's brothers were unreliable. The accounts were poorly maintained, making it difficult to figure out what was due to her. While considering taking legal action, she sensed the need for an alternative source of income. So she applied for the job of Urdu teacher at a progressive school and got it because of her academic background and a successful interview.

The experience was liberating. With her new-found independence there was time to reflect on other needs – something she was not accustomed to doing. At the same time, she had misgivings. It occurred to her that a host of opportunities may have slipped by with the passage of time.

'What're you thinking about, Mama?' Raina, her eldest asked as they drove home after an outing.

'Nothing really … making plans, I guess.'

'About what?'

'Your studies … the future.'

'Marriage … possibly?' Raina enquired with a smile.

'Too early for that, but, yes, one day we'll have to work on that too.'

'We'll manage, Mama,' said Saima, the second daughter.

'Of course, we will.'

She felt reassured by the girls' confidence in her.

Meher organized her affairs with quiet efficiency. Family life with the girls took priority. Teaching became a vocation. She revived ties with the NGO and learnt to play bridge.

By the time the girls had grown, Meher had become principal of the school and director of the NGO. She had gained public recognition as an educationist and human rights campaigner and was often invited to speak at seminars and conferences. Although in her early forties, she had regained much of her earlier attractiveness. She felt and looked younger.

❀

Finances at the NGO were a constant cause of concern. Scanning her tabletop for donors, Meher accessed an online forum called 'Humanaid'. She saw a message on the site from a user called Manfriend: 'Is there anyone out there? I seek a touch of humanity.'

Struck by the extravagant tone of the appeal, she impulsively wrote back, 'How about a worthy project addressing human needs?'

'What kind of needs?' came the response.

'Primary need: funds for securing the rights of poor women with legal problems. Secondary need: administrative services for such matters.'

'No cash, but jack of all trades. Help possible if cause acceptable.'

'Come see for yourself, with credentials.'

'Where, when, who?'

'Tell me about yourself first.'

'First you, then me.'

'Not in this for playing games,' she wrote, logging off.

At the annual board meeting, the NGO secretary, retired Colonel Jamal Shah, a long-standing colleague of Meher, announced that a notable firm of chartered accountants had offered to provide pro bono services.

Meher was relieved when Salman Ahmed, CA, called the following week. He was around thirty, trendy, evolved, amiable. The books were checked with brisk efficiency. At Meher's suggestion, Salman agreed to streamline office operations and update the IT system. His professionalism was reassuring. Feeling that the administration was in capable hands, Meher resumed her quest for funds.

A few days later, she was startled by a message addressed to her on the forum site, stating, 'Touch of humanity not enough; I crave the milk of human kindness.'

She responded, involuntarily, 'Appalling misuse of Shakespeare. What do you really want?'

'To connect with you.'

'How? You don't know me.'

'I can tell, you're the one who responded earlier.'

'So?'

'So that's a beginning.'

'Not possible to connect.'

'Let's at least chat.'

'For a while perhaps. Chat then.'

'Lonely for real people.'

'What do you do?'

'Work for living. What about you?'

'Mind house and work.'

'Animal, mineral, vegetable?'

'Human.'

'Male, female?'

'Indeterminate.'

'Age?'

'100.'

'Very experienced then?'

'Not really, life's gone by quickly. Seem to have missed out on many things. Hope to catch up.'

'At 100? That's ambitious.'

'Well, perhaps 50.'

'Finally, the truth. Tell me about your regrets.'

'Must go. Bye.'

She signed off abruptly, bewildered by the implications of the exchange, and wondering why she had participated in it.

Her thoughts were interrupted by Jamal Shah's knock.

'Jamal Shah, by the look on your face, it seems we've hit the bottom of the barrel?'

'Almost.'

'How awful!'

'Didn't want to depress you … thought we could take time off by going out for a bite.'

She was about to decline but recalling that it was his wife's death anniversary, said, 'Marvellous … could do with some cheering up … let's go.'

'Do you have any preferences regarding eating places?' Jamal Shah asked Meher while driving to a locale where most of the 'in' eateries were situated.

'Anywhere will do. You decide,' she murmured, struck by the thought that it was her first-ever social outing with a man.

'Have you been to any of the places here?' Jamal Shah enquired, turning into a narrow street lined with cafes, snack bars and restaurants.

'I've been to one or two casual ones for coffee and snacks with the girls.'

'Then we'll avoid the youth spots and pick one for old fogies,' he said, grinning.

'Speak for yourself Jamal Shah.'

'Was doing just that … why, you're anything but a fogey … such vitality … such style… '

'Really, Jamal Shah,' she said, blushing. 'You know, what they say about flattery.'

Jamal Shah stopped at the Zamzama Arms, evidently a new establishment which Meher had not heard of. He handed the car keys to a parking valet, startled Meher by buying a bunch of roses from a tiny street urchin, and escorted her into an art nouveau bistro chock-a-block with Aubrey Beardsley's curvilinear Salomes and Chughtai's dreamy maidens.

'Interesting,' Meher remarked, looking around self-consciously.

When handed the menu, she hummed and hawed, until Jamal Shah took it from her and placed the order. To Meher's surprise, his selection from starter to dessert was unusual and quite enjoyable. He also managed to produce some wine mysteriously – which Meher declined to imbibe. Not Jamal Shah, though. He savoured every mouthful like a connoisseur, rolling it around his tongue before swallowing.

Over coffee, Meher assessed him with new eyes.

'You're wondering about me and the food, et cetera,' he said sheepishly.

'Well, yes.' She nodded. 'I've known you for ages, we worked together closely … never seen this side of you.'

'I was military attaché at our embassy in Paris. French cuisine was a passion. My wife and I dined at different places whenever we could, being forced to live on bread and cheese for the remainder of the week.

'Sounds like fun.'

'It was. We also took cookery courses … as a matter of fact, I have cordon bleu rating.'

'My word! I'd never have suspected.'

'I'll prepare a meal for you one day, and then you can judge.'

'I'd like that. But how come no one knows about this?'

'I don't talk about it … not after my wife passed away…' He looked at his hands, then said, 'I've avoided cooking since … I don't mind talking to you. Helps bring it out.' Pausing to sip wine, he said finally, 'I haven't dined out like this in ages.'

Meher watched him silently, at a loss for words.

'There has to be a new beginning at some point,' he continued, addressing himself rather than Meher. 'This, I suppose, is a good time for it.'

Sensing the direction the conversation was taking, Meher reached for her handbag and said, 'Jamal Shah, we've had a pleasant evening. I've come to know you better … and shared some of your private moments. Don't be gloomy, not tonight anyway. We'll talk about these matters another time.'

❀

Manfriend carried on pursuing Meher. She was intrigued by his periodic messages, but did not respond to them.

'Wonder about the private life of a private person like you,' he wrote on one occasion.

'Why don't you let me in?' he enquired on another.

'I'll huff and puff and blow your cover away, and have you for dinner,' was the last cryptic message.

Since the online chatting occurred in the public domain, she was concerned lest other forum members who knew her username came upon the messages.

'Stop haranguing me,' she typed peevishly.

'I will, if you agree to chat privately.'

'I don't have time for all this.'

'Please don't go away.'

'Go away from who or what?'

'I know, you're a woman with deep feelings.'

'A woman – how can you tell and how do you presume about my feelings?'

'I know, I know, I'm picky about the company I keep. Do you have any ties, any commitment that may be compromised by chatting with me?'

'Of course not. None of your business anyway.'

'Then what's the problem?'

'What can possibly come of this?'

'Does something have to come of it? Why can't we just be two individuals talking to each other across the world?'

Yes, she thought, *why not?*

It was a new experience, being sought in that manner – by a strange man.

Hearing a knock on the door, Meher logged off the chat line. Her PA came in with draft accounts prepared by

Salman. Despite the lack of funds, she was pleased with the smooth running of the office since Salman's coming. She dialled his extension to clarify some remarks in the accounts. He responded.

After a pause, he said, 'I read in the morning papers that you've left the school.'

'Not quite left … retired would be more appropriate.'

'That's good, because this place needs more of your time.'

'Really?' she remarked.

'Well … you're the moving spirit of the organization.'

On an impulse, she asked, 'What would it cost to engage your services twice a week?'

'Are you bent on bankrupting the poor NGO? Why do you want to pay for something I'm happy to do for free?'

She was impressed by his sense of commitment.

※

Her private chat sessions with Manfriend became a regular feature. Their association was surreal. They met in a rarefied sphere. Occasional references to home and the workplace made for common ground. Manfriend came across as enlightened, youngish, single, funny and caring. He desired a long-term association. Meher was more circumspect. Warding off intimacy, she spoke of her 'greater maturity', 'family ties' and 'blighted past'. Connectivity was an exciting experience for her. She looked forward to each chat session with a girlish enthusiasm.

One day he suggested they meet. She had been anticipating this, but recoiled at the prospect.

'Why so silent?' he asked. 'Do you have reservations?'

'I have to think about it.'

She came back in a while. 'I am a widow with growing children. Always have to consider how my conduct will affect them.'

He did not respond. The silence gnawed. She felt she had lost him and panicked. Two days later she was tempted to contact him, but resisted the urge. A few more days passed before he returned.

'Would your children object to their extraordinary mother meeting an old friend?'

She smiled, feeling a surge of affection for him.

'I don't think so. But what then?'

'We will have to see.'

We will indeed, she thought, puzzled by how a casual encounter had the makings of a relationship. *What were his expectations?*

Sensing a kind of awakening within, she was wary of overplaying her hand and also feared facing any kind of exposure. Yet she was unwilling to give him up. She wanted the arm's-length arrangement to continue but suspected that the urge to meet would ultimately prevail.

Meher was preoccupied when Jamal Shah came into her office.

'Still fretting over money?' he enquired.

'No ... awesome personal problems.'

'Oh, any way I can be of help?'

'That's nice of you, Jamal Shah,' she said, touched by his concern. 'It's far too personal for anyone but me to sort out ... if you see what I mean.'

'Didn't mean to pry,' he said self-consciously.

'Never mind. We've been colleagues for years, worked through many projects, for me to question your interest in my affairs.'

'By the way,' Jamal Shah continued, anticipating the reason for her concern, 'do you know that Raina has been coming here?'

'I had some idea. I was hoping she'd take an interest in office work other than simply tagging along when I interviewed women prisoners. How is she doing?'

'You'll have to see for yourself.'

The situation became clear when Meher turned up one afternoon while Raina was at the NGO. Meher found her chatting animatedly with Salman over tea and biscuits. By the look of things, they seemed more than passing acquaintances. At the time, Meher felt a pang of something she had not experienced before.

Later, she put it down to maternal cautiousness and curiosity about Salman's motives. She had some reservations concerning her daughter's interest in her colleagues but found nothing objectionable in Salman. On hindsight, she felt that someone like him would probably work well for Raina despite the age difference. Yet she suspected that she had been kept in the dark by design. This bothered her. So she decided to get to the bottom of it.

On Salman's next call at her office, Meher made passing reference to the problems of bringing up a young family, then turning to him, remarked, 'I believe you know Raina.'

'Raina?' He puzzled over the name momentarily. 'Why, yes of course, I came upon her when she was here, at your behest I assumed, to learn about victimized women seeking justice. She's a delightful young lady ... makes us laugh ... and brings us delicious snacks,' he said matter-of-factly. 'Do you know why I am drawn to her?'

Meher peered closely for some giveaway sign of interest in Raina.

'She reminds me of a niece,' he said with a distant look, 'who was a part of our family, until my sister and brother-in-law swooped down and took her off to Canada.'

'So, dear child, you've discovered Salman,' Meher said to Raina later that evening.

Raina at nineteen was a prettier version of Meher. She had a fairly mature approach to life owing to the uncertain times her family had faced following her father's death.

'Yes, I met him when I went to the office looking for you a while back,' she replied casually, 'but you weren't there.'

'Why didn't you call before coming?'

'It was a spur of the moment thing … I wanted to surprise you. A college friend dropped me. Our project supervisor had suggested we do a research paper on women prisoners for the semester.'

'I see.'

'I was meant to ask you to arrange a tour. So I decided to come by and get your approval. Not finding you or Uncle Jamal Shah and no car to take me home, I waited in your office. I was going through those pictures of the women prisoners with babies – the ones you brought home – when Salman came in. He wondered what I was doing there. When I told him, he offered his car and driver to take me home.'

'That's it?'

'The rest you know, Mama.'

The ringing of the telephone interrupted the discussion. Raina answered it. Jamal Shah was calling for Meher.

Meher took the receiver, frowning slightly at what

Jamal Shah had to say. He invited her to a dinner which he would prepare, at his home, on an evening of her choice, the following week. Jamal Shah's invitation had come sooner than expected. She was not prepared for it. She was not sure how to respond. Raina noted her mother's uneasiness.

After deliberating a while Meher said, 'That's very kind of you ... you sure you can manage all four of us? Yes, four ... me and the girls.'

Jamal Shah confirmed that he could, but clarified that this dinner was meant for her. He would ask the girls another time. There was no way out now, so she parried.

'Will there be other people? I see ... just us ... let me think about it ... I'll get back to you ... no, no, not upset ... a little surprised ... of course you've every right ... you're an old friend, after all.'

The telephone call was ill timed. It was an awkward moment for Meher and Raina.

'It's all right, Mama,' Raina said reassuringly, venturing into hitherto unexplored territory, 'for Uncle Jamal Shah to be concerned about you. You're always working, always alone, nice if you could settle down.'

Meher looked at Raina, at a loss for words. They had never spoken on such matters before.

Finally, she said, 'But, I'm leading a settled life.'

'Didn't mean that, Mama. You and Uncle Jamal Shah look good together...'

'Stop,' Meher interjected. 'He's a colleague and a friend ... in that order ... that's all ... anyway it's too late for me to think of such things.'

'What do you mean too late? Take a look at yourself.'

'I'd rather look at you.'

'Mama, please...'

'Raina, I've no romantic inclinations, never had, so drop the subject.'

Somewhat disappointed, Raina turned to go but Meher stopped her: 'It's your turn now,' she said, conscious that a change had taken place in their relationship. For the moment, they were no longer mother and daughter, but two women having a one-on-one.

'Is there anything I need to know about Salman and you?'

'No, Mama no,' Raina said, recalling Meher's look of bewilderment when she came upon her chatting with Salman. 'I guess I was drawn to him at first. So, I went to the office a few times laden with snacks for the staff, but he was ... almost avuncular ... treated me as a younger person ... usually left me chatting with Uncle Jamal Shah and other staff members. That's all.'

After a pause, Meher said, 'When you do take an interest in anyone ... you will let me know, won't you?'

'I will Mama, I will. And when you develop an interest … I assume you'll tell me,' Raina shot back.

Meher laughed and nodded her head.

❋

Meher came upon Jamal Shah and Salman discussing NGO matters in her office.

'Good news,' Jamal Shah said, 'we've got a grant from Belgium.'

'Not to forget the official Australian offer,' Salman added.

'Saved by the bell … where's the paperwork?'

'On your table,' Jamal Shah said as they left the room. 'Call if you need me.'

She had barely settled down when 'Knock! Knock! Knock! Anyone there?' flashed on the tabletop screen.

'You can do better than that,' she remarked.

'What about our chat away from virtual reality?' he persisted. 'The slings and arrows of outrageous fortune are nothing compared to what I would suffer.'

'Any more blank verse from you and that will be the end of this conversation.'

'But seriously, have you thought of meeting up with me?'

'I have, but am still unsure.'

'Unsure of what? My friendship, commitment,

devotion?' he sounded impatient. She turned away from the screen.

Here it comes, she thought, *the outpouring ... claims ... demands ... needs ... yearnings.*

Numerous questions came to mind about them together. What direction would their association take once they met? Would they maintain privacy or be upfront? How would she put it to her daughters? What would relatives say? Would it affect her public image?

She returned to the computer undecided about her reply. Another message flashed on the screen, 'Stop agonizing. I know who you are.'

Ambushed, trapped, she wondered how she had been discovered. Trying to guess who it might be, she spied the table calendar. It had been left open on a day nine months earlier. On the page relating to that day, she had scrawled: *Manfriend's first call*. Under that, there was an updated note in a different hand: *I believe, 'am finally in touch with humanity*. The writing was not Jamal Shah's.

There was a sound at the door. She looked up. Salman stood there watching her quizzically, a smile playing on his lips.

Two Is an Odd Number

They made an unusual couple. She was tall and svelte with chiselled features, held doctorates from Harvard and Cambridge in philosophy and jurisprudence and had a purposeful way about her. Talal was smaller, plumpish and homely with dark brown hair and smiling eyes. He was 'Urdu-speaking', enjoyed poetry and was easy-going.

Their first meeting was coincidental. They had adjoining seats on a flight from London to Karachi. As the plane took off, Yasmin paled and lapsed into prayer. From his aisle seat, he took in the stylish suit, casually draped scarf, and murmuring red lips. When her incantation failed to end, he interrupted her gently.

'What is it?' she asked testily.

'Drinks … drinks…' he muttered lamely, indicating the trolley.

'I can see … are you trying to sell them to me?'

Talal slunk back into his seat, chastened.

She noted the serge shalwar kurta, worsted waistcoat, fingers running through an unruly little beard and Ahmad Faraz's poems alongside a pad on the service table.

When the evening meal was being served, Yasmin asked for red wine. As she was sipping it, the plane lurched, making her spill some on Talal. She apologized repeatedly, at pains to dab the mess out of sight. After an awkward pause, he got up and told her not to fret as he enjoyed the occasional dousing in wine.

Yasmin slept all the way to Karachi. When collecting her things before disembarking, she noticed the Faraz book in the seat pocket. Glimpsing Talal as he was about to leave the baggage terminal, she hurried towards him, waving the book.

'I thought you were about to attack me,' he said teasingly.

❋

Yasmin was coming home from the US after a nervous breakdown. Her friend and mentor, Dr Ruth Summerland, had found her at a computer in a flood of tears. According to Ruth it was time for Yasmin, at thirty-five, to go back home and take stock. And of course it was. Yasmin had spent fifteen years of her life in academe,

and barely noticed. She had been attracted for a while
to a Bosnian scholar, and then to a Swedish doctor who
had converted to Islam. Dimly aware of being frigid, she
decided instead to carry on as a single woman. In the
meantime, trying to keep the conflict within at bay had
brought on the present crisis.

Her mother, sensing the change in Yasmin, managed to
convince her that marriage may be the solution. Finding
a prospective husband for Yasmin was a difficult task
given her age, liberal outlook and academic baggage.
Her parents were upper-middle-class bureaucrats – a
criterion that mattered while on the lookout for potential
matches.

❧

Talal was the editor of an Urdu newspaper and a member
of the committee that selected poetry for the annual
publication of the National Academy of Letters. He was
one of the six children of a judge of the Small Claims
Court. While his siblings were married, Talal, at thirty-
three, was still a bachelor. Many members of his family
had emigrated due to the uncertainties plaguing the
country. When his last brother was about to leave, Talal
found himself dreading the thought of a silent house.

But all this was to change. The annual dinner of the
National Academy of Letters set the scene. Talal was
taken by surprise when Yasmin suddenly walked in with

her parents in a midnight-blue sari. They were seated at the same table. During dinner someone knocked over a glass. Both burst into laughter. It was a plausible beginning.

❧

Marriage came about almost as a matter of course. Talal accepted a job offer as the Washington-based representative of a syndicate of Urdu newspapers. Yasmin took up a teaching assignment at Georgetown University. They settled down in a red-brick home near the campus.

It was not easy for two such dissimilar lives to coalesce. While they bonded, the differences between them kept coming in the way. Talal held poetry and chat sessions for 'Urdu-speaking' colleagues. Yasmin hosted cocktails for academics. Their preferences clashed. He craved rich spicy food. She was conditioned to a more austere diet. There were problems with music too. She had a thing about opera and abhorred his ghazal recitals. Nothing could make alcohol kosher in his eyes in Ramazan.

Pregnancy was not something that was expected. But it happened and she had to live with it. He was excited, but confused. They sought guidance from a counsellor. Yasmin felt Talal had taken advantage of her. They quarrelled – occasionally at first, then incessantly – stopped physical contact and ended up barely communicating.

A miscarriage turned into an ordeal. Yasmin suffered stoically. He became morose, monosyllabic. Each blamed the other. She went home to recuperate and never returned. He was hostile, not wanting her back. Divorce came as a relief.

❦

Talal moved to London and took over representation of the newspaper syndicate in the UK and EU countries, putting the US behind him.

'You seem more at peace now,' his London-based brother remarked, looking deep into his eyes, 'but why do you keep glancing over my shoulder?'

'I'm more settled   and ... I suppose ... I keep my eyes open for whatever fate has in store,' he joked.

'You've changed somehow,' his brother remarked, eyeing the fitted overcoat and French beard.

'Well, one develops new interests in time. I've been out of Pakistan for a while.'

'I know ... I know ... but I was a little surprised by ... by...'

'By what?'

'The wine you ordered at lunch.'

'Ah, that...' he remarked wistfully.

Despite a busy life, the loneliness he feared caught

up with him. He met a lot of people and looked forward to each encounter. He travelled extensively in Europe, but it was London that drew him. He felt something awaited him there.

One afternoon he caught sight of Yasmin disappearing into Burlington Arcade. He followed instinctively. Not finding her in the colonnade, he searched shops inside, bumping into her at last in a perfumery. He was about to speak when he discovered with a start that it was not Yasmin at all but someone strikingly like her.

'Oh, I'm … I'm so sorry … I mistook you for someone else.'

'Someone you're used to running into, I take it,' she said, flicking her hair.

'Well, it seems to happen … whenever we meet,' he said, shrugging his shoulders.

They laughed at that. He suggested mocha at an espresso bar. They were soon chatting like old friends. Her name was Sheela Shivdasani. She worked for a major dress designer. She had an attractive earthiness quite unlike Yasmin's ethereality. Talal felt more at ease than he had been in a while. They agreed to meet again.

He introduced her to subcontinental music, poetry, art. Her reactions were evasive but refreshing. It was fun being with her. The emptiness was ebbing. At times, she spoke of his 'wistful look'. She noticed it first when they came upon a shop window displaying a mannequin draped in a midnight-blue sari, and later, on passing a poster of *La Traviata* at Leicester Square tube station.

'It's to do with her, isn't it?' she asked.

He looked away.

❧

Yasmin was having a difficult time getting her life together. Being with Talal had changed her. The break-up left her in limbo.

'I am utterly, utterly derailed,' she declared by email to Ruth. 'I don't want to stay here, or work in this environment. I shall never return to Georgetown. I can't see myself waltzing back to you either. Worse, I don't know what I want to do. I am not even the same person. Your lost friend.'

Her mother arranged therapeutic visits to those 'who would understand' in other parts of the country. The results were ironic. At a ghazal recital arranged by friends, Yasmin broke down on hearing Faraz's '*Ranjish hi sahi, dil hi dukhane ke liye aa*'.

During her stay in Lahore, she addressed a few seminars. This helped, prompting her to accept an offer of associate professorship at London University. Within days she was on the podium again.

Ruth was so pleased at Yasmin's recovery that she sent her tickets online for a Verdi opera season at Covent Garden.

While thinking about it, Yasmin got a call from Stockholm. It was her old friend Stefan Lindberg, wanting to say hello. During the conversation, she got carried away and impulsively asked him to join her in London for the opening. So a blonde Stefan, arresting in formal attire, escorted Yasmin in her gold sari to the opera.

The opening bars of *Traviata* were magical. As Yasmin was about to enter a world of romance and tragedy, she saw Talal in a box nearby. She instinctively retreated into the shadows of her box. It was clear that the situation had to be dealt with. In the interval, Talal was not to be seen. When Stefan went to the washroom, she made her way to the packed lounge bar and found Talal in the crowd, holding a glass of champagne. She could tell he was more than just astonished.

'Careful with the bubbly,' she cautioned.

That broke the ice. They looked at each other quizzically. Her attempt to steer the conversation to the matter in mind was cut short by Sheela's 'Hello darling, I'm back.'

'Yasmin,' Talal said, looking away, 'I want you to meet … my wife Sheela.'

The two women sized each other up.

'Wonderful, wonderful,' Yasmin blurted out, 'how very wonderful … so happy for you. You're really quite lovely.'

'No, *you* are,' said Sheela. 'What a surprise meeting you finally … I've heard so much about you.'

'Yasmin,' Stefan called over chattering heads from the doorway, 'time to go in, the second bell's gone.'

'Who's that?' Sheela asked.

'Dr Stefan Lindberg,' Yasmin said in a matter-of-fact way.

'You mean Abu Baqr Lindberg, himself?' Talal asked, eyebrows raised.

Yasmin nodded self-consciously.

As the curtain rose for the next act, Sheela remarked to Talal, 'That was a brutal way to do it.'

'That's the way the cookie crumbles.'

When it was over, the heroine dead, auditorium resounding to a standing ovation, Sheela observed that Yasmin and Stefan looked exceptionally good together.

'Yes,' Talal said ruefully, 'union of a Viking hero with the goddess of the East.'

'My, you are in poetic vein … and … there's that wistful look again.'

❦

Yasmin liked Stefan's suggestion of a marriage ceremony at the Islamic Centre in Regent's Park.

What puzzled her was Stefan's reaction to the champagne with which she toasted him at a postnuptial party.

'But you know I imbibed ... when we dined out on your London visits.'

'That was before you became my wife.'

'What's that supposed to mean?'

'That we're a Muslim couple now ... and that's how we should behave.'

Yasmin's life in Stockholm was marred from the outset by Stefan's extravagant Islamic orthodoxy. It took her completely by surprise. Marriage, for him, was a divine contract. She was especially put out by his sanctimonious approach to sex. He explained away courtship as 'a time of discovery ... it's different now, of course ... we can enjoy being together ... but we must observe the prescribed conduct.'

'What if ... I think differently?'

'There's only one code of conduct ... for the faithful.'

'Concerning relations between husband and wife?'

'Yes.'

'Whatever became of spontaneity?'

'The code deals with everything that matters.'

She felt unable to cope with the situation, so she declined an offer from Uppsala University and reverted to the previous teaching arrangement. When leaving for London, she told Stefan that she understood his commitment to his beliefs but was not sure she was cut out for the part.

'I'll think about it, and if I can resolve it, I'll be back for good.'

'And ... for the time being?' he asked sadly.

'For the time being I'll commute. We've still got a marriage, you know, and we care for each other. But you deserve something better than a non-conformist wife. So we've got to work at it.'

❀

Talal's newspaper syndicate had co-sponsored a rally publicizing the danger to world peace posed by the terrorist threat to Pakistan. A swelling crowd of participants gathered at Speakers Corner awaiting the start of the rally. It had begun to drizzle. Yasmin was there with a group from the university. Stacks of placards provided by the sponsors were depleting rapidly. She reached for one of the last few as did Talal. There was a brief tug of war which ceased abruptly when they recognized each other.

'You look just the same ... pale ... but nicer ... much, much nicer ... How long has it been?'

'Too long to recall ... you also look well ... a little leaner perhaps ... the eyes, more reflective ... but the grey in the beard ... very distinguished.'

'Stefan, or shall I say, Abu Baqr, where is he?'

'In Sweden ... we divorced a while back.'

'I see ... I'm sorry.'

'Don't be ... it was amicable ... and Sheela, how is she?'

'Died eighteen months ago ... cancer.'

'That's awful ... how sad.'

'Awful for her ... sad for me ... but hard work and time have helped.'

They walked with the crowd heading for the West End, talking in snatches. She held up the placard for a while. Then he did. They ended up holding it together.

Missing Person

The boy had been brought back to Karachi suffering from acute emotional distress...

Aamer looked out of the window of the consulting room he shared with a colleague. The view of the world outside had a steadying influence on him. His earlier disquiet had been partially deflected by the summing-up therapy session just concluded with nineteen-year-old Sherzaman Khan.

From the third floor he could see traffic and pedestrians moving laboriously through the narrow lanes that passed for side streets off Zamzama Boulevard.

Spotting the lean figure of Sherzaman disappearing down the road, Aamer recalled the shrivelled human being of the initial sessions.

Sherzaman's mother had approached Aamer through his colleague, Dr Nazli Ashraf, to help deal with a situation that a lower-middle-class family was unable to handle. The father was an ironmonger. The boy, a product of government schooling, had been sent north to a seminary specializing in traditional disciplines and rudimentary commando exercises, from which he was expected to qualify in an increasingly militant environment.

The breakdown had put an end to all that. When Sherzaman was first brought for treatment, Aamer had insisted on a period of hospitalization for tackling his catatonia, a condition Aamer managed to control with the aid of drugs. A few months later, Aamer was able to shift focus to discussion therapy.

Unravelling preliminary layers of the personality exposed an Oedipal complex of resentment towards the father and an obsessive attachment for the mother. Other telling revelations related to experiences at the training institute where the rigours of the regimen were allayed for Sherzaman by the special attention he got from the instructor of his batch. Little gestures of tenderness, preferential treatment in field exercises and sidelong glances exchanged during study sessions occurred with growing frequency, giving rise to knowing winks and nudges amongst the students and turmoil in the mind of Sherzaman, who experienced emotional and physical reactions of an unusual nature.

The implications of the situation were not lost on

Aamer who was reminded of an early episode in his own life concerning an overbearing PT instructor. But Sherzaman's predicament was something more than mere boyish stirrings triggered by teenage hormones.

On a late-night training manoeuvre conducted in border territory, a small band of trainees led by the instructor was taken unawares by hostile firing from unknown quarters. While his comrades scrambled for cover, Sherzaman fell to the ground, cowering and sobbing uncontrollably, until carried by the instructor to shelter behind a rock outcropping. They lay there together until dawn when the instructor considered it safe to reassemble the scattered band and retreat. The experience precipitated Sherzaman's breakdown and eventual return to Karachi – a blubbering heap propped and prodded by two seminarians.

When Dr Nazli first discussed the case with Aamer, she was not too clear about the facts. She had to rely on the garbled version narrated by Sherzaman's mother, who had based her account on what the pair of seminarians saw fit to reveal. Despite the somewhat convoluted picture that emerged, both Nazli and Aamer were sufficiently familiar with Freudian analyses to identify the true nature of Sherzaman's psychosis.

It came as no surprise to Aamer that Sherzaman's conservative family was not fully apprised about the cause of his predicament.

'Aren't you going to tell them?' Aamer asked cautiously.

'Not me ... they've been shielded from it all along ... such subjects are abhorrent to their kind. If they knew, God knows how they would react,' Nazli said.

'Nor how they would interact with Sherzaman,' Aamer murmured.

'The seminary representatives who accompanied him,' Nazli continued, 'were emphatic that factors such as rigours of training, spartan living conditions, fierce student competitiveness, practising with dangerous weapons, none of which suited Sherzaman's gentle temperament, were the likely causes of his breakdown.'

'How about the instructor's role?' Aamer queried. 'I'd call that a major contributory factor. Wouldn't you?'

'His involvement has been glossed over by the seminary authorities.'

'*Munafiqeen*,' Aamer uttered under his breath.

'What was that?' Nazli asked.

'Just calling them by their correct name – hypocrites.'

'Yes, I suppose hypocrisy is a convenient option for most people promoting a lifestyle governed by dogma.'

'Right ... while you, Nazli, and I have to deal with the real McCoy, the parents and instructors prefer to believe that there is no such thing.'

※

With his consultancy period for the day almost at an end, Aamer returned to the desk to enter his summary on Sherzaman's file.

The subject, he wrote, *attended the summing-up session without his father who apparently has little appreciation for psychotherapy*. As he wrote he remembered how Sherzaman's angular face shadowed by a fledgling beard remained apprehensive all through the discussion, his gold-flecked eyes watching Aamer closely when he discussed his findings in mixed English and Urdu.

References to Sherzaman's relationship with his father were met with hostility followed by expressions of incredulity when Aamer hinted at the implications of the boy's special feelings for his mother. But when Aamer broached the subject of his sexual inclinations, darkness relieved by glimmerings of comprehension fell across Sherzaman's even features.

In measured tones, Aamer had explained that if he was not averse to sleeping with women, Sherzaman could opt for a straight lifestyle by curbing his homosexual tendencies. The alternative was of course, a gay life, which in an orthodox milieu was unlawful and entailed clandestine sex with impermanent partners. The third option was what Aamer called 'a bit of both', practised openly with attendant complications, or hypocritically in camera.

At the end of the session, Aamer took a deep breath and asked Sherzaman if he had any questions. A clearly moved Sherzaman did not reply. Instead, he grasped Aamer's hand and raised it to his forehead.

'Doctor Sahib,' he remarked with a catch in his voice, 'you've made me aware of many things I needed to know. Yes, I do understand … I think for the first time I understand clearly.' Then he was gone.

❦

A buzz on the intercom was followed by a voice announcing that Dr Nazli had arrived for her evening consultations. Aamer glanced at his watch and put away his files and medical reports in a wall cabinet. He was about to leave when the door opened on Begum Safia Mirza, his adoptive mother, bearing a birthday cake topped with forty-six lit candles. She was followed by staff members on duty and a reluctant Dr Nazli, who had been persuaded by Safia to join the party.

Aamer's bewildered protests were drowned out by the strains of 'Happy Birthday' sung by a chorus of dissonant voices. After a brief flurry of festivity during which the candles were blown out and slivers of cake distributed, Nazli discreetly led the staff out of the room to allow Aamer some privacy with Safia Mirza.

To Aamer, Safia was 'special'. She had been a close friend of Aamer's late mother and mother-in-law. A childless widow, Safia looked on Aamer and his wife Zara with something akin to a maternal eye, claiming to have been responsible for bringing them together – even though Aamer and Zara's marriage was the outcome of a love affair that had begun while they were both at university in New York.

Safia's slightly intrusive visit brought back the uneasy feeling Aamer had experienced earlier that day. What in other circumstances would have been agreeable enough was marred by the realization that Safia had come there not to surprise but remind him of the decisions he had to make.

'Delighted to see you, Khalajan,' Aamer said. 'But why all the fuss?'

'How else could I get to see you?' Safia countered. 'You've been avoiding me.'

'Not here, not now,' Aamer interrupted. 'It's Dr Nazli's turn to use this room. Her patients are waiting.'

'You're putting me off again,' Safia protested.

Aamer steered Safia out of the room, through the reception area occupied by Nazli's patients and a somewhat disconcerted receptionist into the staff lounge.

Once inside, Aamer closed the door firmly and made Safia sit in a chair. Facing her with his back to the window, he shot a remark at her. 'You want me to return home to make it all right again ... so you can feel good about it.'

'Stop it!' she said shrilly. 'Stop going on about what I want. The point is what're you going to do about the mess you've made?'

'*I've* made?'Aamer asked incredulously.

'Well, you chose to leave Zara. Naturally she must share the responsibility, but you could have settled the matter at home instead of dashing off to the club and making the whole world witness the rupture of the so-called ideal couple.'

That was the sticking point. By walking out of the house he had precipitated the crisis. He was being blamed for the split.

❈

Safia's allusion to the 'ideal couple' brought back the past. What a cliché, he mused, and yet how true. That's how friends at university and, later, relatives at their wedding had seen them. It was also the way in which Zara and he had inevitably come to regard themselves. When the twins were born the charmed circle was complete.

They had met as undergraduates for the first time while visiting university friends at Martha's Vineyard that Labor Day weekend twenty-five years ago. Being the only Pakistanis at the day-long get-together organized by beachfront residents, natural curiosity had drawn them together. An exchange of prefatory remarks had led to the discovery of the long-standing friendship between their mothers.

All day they had sat facing each other against a backdrop of changing colours mirrored by the sky and sea, undisturbed by their friends who could sense what was happening.

❋

Aamer's thoughts were interrupted by Safia saying with a tinge of nostalgia, 'But your marriage was ... was simply perfect.'

'Perhaps ... although things were not quite as perfect as they looked.' Aamer paused. 'It was the promotional services company that did it. That's when the rot set in.'

'That was your fault – encouraging her to take on such an ambitious project.'

'All those successful business women's awards – for product promotion, publication, film-making – came in the way, I suppose.' Zara's clientele had ranged from Bill Gates to the Saudi royals for her environment protection programme: her international stature signified by a UN citation. Her success had pleased Aamer initially.

'I was truly proud of her, Khalajan,' he said. Then he added with a smile, 'Top of the pops.'

'What was that?' Safia asked

'Oh, something trivial.'

'Then what was the problem? Another person?'

'Oh no, nothing like that. You see from the beginning I had encouraged her to be her own person ... an individual operating in her space.'

'Operating in her space!' Safia said with disbelief. 'You make her sound robotic ... I thought you cared for her.'

'Can't two individuals be as one when in love ... sharing a life together ... yet conscious of their separate identities?'

'That must've been hard for her,' Safia ventured. 'She really loved you.'

'You mean I didn't? You're wrong there. I felt that if I let her give me all she had to offer, she would be missing out on the success she was capable of.'

'So you pushed her away.'

'It wasn't quite so brutal,' Aamer emphasized. 'I merely guided her to do what she was best at.'

'Yes, yes, I remember your dear mother going on about you doing a Pygmalion on poor Zara. We thought it charming at the time ... and a bit dotty!'

At least that was how it had been in the early years. By the time their sons were halfway through secondary school, Aamer could see only too clearly that his makeover of Zara had created a gulf between them. Anniversary deadlines were either missed or met by one or other, or both of them flying to rendezvous spots in different parts of the world. Holidays with the boys had to be arranged months in advance. Even their time in Karachi was marked by recurring absences of either partner. So Aamer, half-sensing a threat to the marriage, found himself altering his professional commitments to make more time for Zara.

'I opted out of several teaching commitments, Khalajan,' Aamer said, breaking the silence.

'That was *generous* of you,' Safia taunted, 'but still, there were the trips abroad.'

'Yes, brief visits for updating oneself on developments in psychiatry – a must for specialists in my profession.'

'Even so, when you weren't working, you were occupied with strange things ... hobnobbing with sufis ... conducting seminars and publishing articles on faith and what not.'

'Doesn't that tell you something about what I was going through ... while still making time for Zara?'

'Didn't she respond to that?' Safia asked drily.

'Not initially ... she heard what I had to say, and I think she did try, but there was always something else preoccupying her.'

It was at the Master's tea at Trinity College, following the boys' graduation at Cambridge that Zara finally confessed to Aamer about wanting to return to the role of a wife instead of carrying on as a publicist at large.

Aamer chose not to tell Safia about his reaction to Zara's disclosure: he had come to accept Zara's occasional presence as the normal thing.

Instead, he said, 'By the time we got back to Karachi, we were simply out of sync.'

'But things couldn't have been so dreadful ... to have made you leave the house at dead of night?'

Aamer turned away from Safia and looked out of the window at Zamzama Boulevard, darkened by evening shadows.

He spoke half to himself, 'She was so pale that night ... yet lovely. She wanted to talk about recovering what we had lost. She mentioned common interests, mutual friends, plans for the boys. But none of that mattered to me any more, not the interests or plans or friends. I was headed somewhere else. I was looking at me ... for me ... I mean myself. Zara went on and on, she just wouldn't stop. It was clear that we weren't gelling. I had no choice but to get away.'

It was then that Aamer noticed Safia had left.

❀

Peering into the reception area, he caught sight of Nazli's crisp sari-clad figure in the doorway of the consulting room. Aamer had become more conscious of her since their involvement in Sherzaman's case.

He recalled how their discussions on Sherzaman held during evening hours at the consulting chambers were frequently continued at one of the Zamzama coffee bars. On a few occasions they had even extended into late suppers at Nazli's minimalist duplex off Queen's Road. He remembered how the first supper was interrupted by a curly haired girl of five who stood in an archway sucking her thumb. Nazli picked her up, introduced her to him as 'Poppet', before taking her back to bed. Until then he was not aware Nazli had a family.

'I don't,' she said firmly. 'Poppet's the only one. Her father went to Malaysia to research tropical viruses, and opted to stay on with a new Malay wife.'

※

Discovering Aamer having tea later that evening in the staff lounge, Nazli remarked, 'I saw Sherzaman leave the building as I drove to work.'

'How did he look … to you?' Aamer asked anxiously.

'He virtually swooped down on me, waving his hands, beaming, his hair flying in the air like … like a wild bird, so I had to pull over to the kerb. When he came up to the car he said, *Doctor Sahiba … Doctor Sahiba, I feel free … free from pain and confusion … from darkness and guilt.* So I asked him what he was going to do with his new-found freedom. He said, more seriously this time, *I have to make a choice.* After which he laughed and said,

I think I have made my choice. And then ... he kind of disappeared.'

Aamer's spirits lightened. Leaving the building that night, he toyed with the idea of seeing Zara but thought better of it, deciding to go to the club instead. He reflected on the events of the day, realizing that choices had to be made. As he approached his car he skipped involuntarily, more or less echoing Sherzaman's words with sudden, compelling clarity, *I think I've made my choice*.

Unfinished Mural

On the opening day of the exhibition of his paintings, Jibran was woken up at 4 p.m. by Bua, the housekeeper.

'Time to get up,' she said, tweaking his toe.

'But I went to sleep at midday,' he murmured wearily.

'Too bad ... you've got to be at the gallery in an hour.'

She raised the studio blinds and shooed the cat away from Jibran's side.

'You're much too hard on it. Mother loved cats, you know.'

'I know, I know,' said Bua, turning the daybed deftly into a bolstered divan. 'But her pets knew their place, unlike this one ... leaping about, climbing curtains, clawing prayer mats. Remember how they sat, still as statues, outside her room on the last day. It was an amazing sight.'

He did remember. He touched her wedding ring – which he wore on a chain around his neck – recalling the coffin being escorted out of the house by a furry phalanx of seven felines, of which six did not return.

'Only this one came back,' he said, opening the door to let it in before Bua could object.

The exhibition was held at Veena Rahman's gallery. Veena, a divorcee, carried a torch for Jibran. They had been lovers, and were at one stage headed for marriage. His mother had put an end to that by threatening to leave the house if Veena walked in. The unusual bond between mother and son was more than a match for Veena. She had no option except to withdraw, but remained committed to Jibran. She was friend, counsellor and comforting shoulder on at least two later occasions when Jibran had to forgo other likely partners, all because of his mother.

Several canvases at the exhibition contained variations of the mother and child theme. Astute viewers saw a resemblance to Jibran in the hirsute figures shown bursting through female torsos or exploding in wombs. Somewhat self-consciously, Veena compared 'the development of foetuses from the maternal mélange' in

Jibran's work to 'the struggle for attaining human form' discernible in Michelangelo's marble giants of the Boboli Gardens.

The exhibition – the first to be held since his mother's death – was well received but there was something unresolved about the work.

Many were especially intrigued by a layered panel. This showed a large hazy face with glowing eyes, crisscrossed by a variety of felines at different levels and overlaid in the foreground by random leopard spots.

'What's this?' Veena asked, peering at the hazy face. 'The new flavour of the month?'

'Bitchy,' Jibran remarked.

'Catty, sweetheart, would be more appropriate.'

'Stop it, Veena, it's the icon piece I'm working on for the Mohenjodaro mound mural.'

'Ah, the masterpiece you've been doing for ages.'

'No point talking to you when you're in that frame of mind.'

'No, seriously, I'll behave, but tell me about the project, since you won't let me see it.'

'Come to the house on Saturday ... five-ish ... I've asked Alina to tea ... that's her name ...'

'You mean cat-face's name?'

'Veena...' Jibran chided, 'I want you to meet her ... and if you're civil to her, I may even show you my work.'

'Can't wait.'

❈

Jibran would have liked to serve tea in the studio, but Bua preferred the sitting room. The resinous wooden floor, deep enveloping sofas, the Dresden clock – all belonged to his mother. To get over feeling like an intruder, he glanced sideways through sliding doors framing the garden at the herbal beds once tended lovingly by her. A sudden wave-like undulation of staring eyes in what he thought was a still glass panel startled him. But when he looked again nothing other than the derelict beds were visible through the transparent glass. Just then he felt Veena behind him.

'Caught you … out of your shell … your studio, that is,' she teased, putting her arms around his waist.

Still shaken by what he had seen – or imagined – he tried regaining composure by focusing on Veena's reflection in the glass.

'Even though she's not here now, one can feel her presence,' Veena remarked, alluding to the Bevan Petman portrait of his mother. 'Strange, being in this house again.' She shuddered. 'Let's get out of here and go see the hidden wonder.' She felt him stiffen. 'What's the matter, Jibran?'

'Nothing,' he said, patting her hand.

He was put off by her hostility towards his mother. It gave him a reason for not showing her the mural.

He tried to pull away, but stopped short when Veena's reflection in the glass seemed to splinter distortedly like a mirror image disintegrating into fragments. He stared, transfixed. This time he saw the cat scuffling at the sliding doors staring back at him.

The atmosphere lightened when Alina came in with an escort. Her companion, whose looks and manner were impeccable, was introduced as Tariq Fazalbhoy of Fazalbhoy Electronics. Jibran was put out by Tariq's unexpected presence, but said nothing.

With tea over, the group drifted outdoors. Alina wanted to show Tariq around the house. Veena raised her eyebrows in mock surprise at Alina's familiarity with the house. To distract her, Jibran took Veena for a stroll through wild and wasted vegetation leading to a simulated baroque fish pool. It was adorned with stone cherubs pouring water from urns and conch shells spurting jets. Cascades spouted from concealed fountains and streams flowed down ferny rocks. It was an ideal habitat for the fish gliding through the dappled waters.

When they approached the spot, Veena felt Jibran hesitate, but she held his arm and urged him on.

'Mother spent most evenings here, until it was time to go,' he said distractedly, touching the wedding ring.

'Did she? Then you should come here more often, to keep the memory alive.'

'What if … what if I….'

'What?'

'Want to forget?'

'Then she would truly die. Why would you want to kill an important part of your life?'

He looked quizzically at her. 'You're quite something, you know … something wise and wonderful … you are concerned about her even though she hurt you.'

She pressed his hand. They leaned against each other, taking in the scents and sounds of the still garden.

As the shadows lengthened, Alina and Tariq joined them.

'It's so … so … jewel like.' Alina remarked delightedly, bending down to look at the fish.

There was a momentary silence interrupted by sounds of splashing water.

'Magical,' Tariq murmured involuntarily, 'quite … quite magical … as if touched by an enchanter.'

Alina looked up intrigued and moved closer to him. Jibran noticed their hands touch, seemingly by accident, and remain together. He felt a twinge – was it, could it be – of jealousy. He dismissed the thought, but was overcome by the despair of someone about to lose a game. He sensed that if she was prevented somehow from posing for the mural, it would be a great loss for the project – and for him personally.

A movement in the shrubbery interrupted Jibran's

train of thought. In an opening among the trees, the rays of the setting sun lit up a slowly rotating object – it was his mother's wheelchair. He clutched at Veena, pointing a shaking forefinger at the opening. Tariq bounded towards it and came upon the cat leaping like a phantom from bush to bush after an unseen quarry. No wheelchair was to be seen.

'Time to go in,' Veena said, supporting Jibran.

As they turned to leave, instant illumination flooded the site. Bua, or someone else in the house, had switched on the battery of lights around the pool. There was stunned silence. The extraordinary setting dispelled the apprehension aroused by the earlier event.

'Magnificent,' Tariq remarked, studying the intricate layout of the pool lights. 'So well designed ... this lighting arrangement ... creates dream-like illusions ... absolutely fascinating,'

Just then there was an explosive crackle followed by a hissing sound. The lights blinked, sputtered and went out. A smell of singed rubber lingered.

'Short circuit,' said Jibran.

'Shame,' said Tariq.

'Enough surprises for one evening,' Veena said, leading Jibran firmly from the darkened pool towards the house.

Most of the house was without electricity. Tariq

offered to check the circuits, but his proposal was frostily declined by Jibran.

'It's too much of an imposition, expecting you to do that.'

'Not at all,' Tariq persisted. 'Circuitry is something I'm good at.'

'No, no, it would be too bothersome.'

'You're being silly, Jibran,' Veena said. 'Why don't you let him try?'

Jibran found Tariq's presence irksome. He wanted him to leave.

But Tariq did try, and brought electricity back to the house.

'Tomorrow, I'll return,' he said, looking squarely at Jibran, 'and with your permission, I'll repair the pool lighting system.'

'Are you serious?' Jibran asked incredulously.

'Nothing but—' he said with barely concealed excitement.

'Let him do it,' Alina pleaded.

'Of course he will,' Veena confirmed.

❋

A viscous mixture of colours seems to merge, separate, flow into one another, forming a mask that spins on a pivot ... it reveals a different visage as it rotates ...

Veena's even features ... Bua's creased look ... a blank ... a barely discernible face ... then Alina's radiance ...

Jibran stirred restlessly in bed. The cat lying alongside stretched its legs and rolled over, paws in the air.

A wheelchair approaches a giant mural of the Mound of the Dead topped by a cluster of stars ... the mound is inscribed with pictographs, calligraphy, graffiti, abstract images ... the apex icon of the mound with the all-seeing eye, held aloft by the dancing girl, breaks off ... it tumbles down landing in the wheelchair ... the wheelchair disappears swiftly in a maze of greenery ... the mural disintegrates...

Jibran sat up, took a sip of water and dozed off again.

Cats of all sizes converge on a shining mirror fish skim the surface ... they leap about to escape predatory paws and snapping jaws amidst flashes of light ... the cats vanish leaving fish bones in a mound-like arrangement on the mirror's surface ...

Jibran got hastily out of bed and wiped the sweat off his forehead. He felt threatened. To escape from sinister dreams, he focused on reading.

❦

An exhausted Jibran slept till lunchtime. He had forgotten Tariq's offer to repair the pool lighting system and was surprised to find him at the fish pool, tinkering with the waterworks. Bua had let him in. Jibran regarded Tariq as an intruder but felt it was too late to stop him.

He retired to the studio, coming out occasionally to observe Tariq's progress from the safe distance of the veranda. Tariq worked rapidly: transferring the fish to a barrel, draining and cleaning the pool, disassembling pumps and lighting system, attending to the electrical work. Bua's approval of his efforts was met with scorn from Jibran.

'He's far too cocky, too full of himself,' Jibran remarked. But he sensed that there was something 'special' about Tariq.

By dusk, Jibran noted that most of the work had been done. In the growing darkness, he could see Tariq barefoot in shallow residual water, hurriedly finishing tasks that had to be completed before bulk water could be released and the fish returned to their habitat.

'I'm eager to see it in full glory,' Tariq called out. 'Aren't you?'

'Get on with it', Jibran replied. 'Then begone!' he muttered under his breath.

'Must finish waterproofing the leads before switching on the power, otherwise the water will become electrically charged,' Tariq explained.

Ignoring him, Jibran agitatedly paced the veranda from the switchboard end to the other. After some time, he saw Bua making her way towards Tariq with tea and biscuits. Suddenly, the pool lights came on and blood-curdling shrieks pierced the stillness. Bua dropped the tray and Jibran stopped in his tracks, petrified. Both stared in horror at the convulsed, contorted, animated figure in the pool – leaping, twisting, jerking, flaring like a scarecrow on fire – crumple into a smouldering, smoking heap. Then there was darkness, silence and the sickly, sweet odour of burnt human flesh.

It was never clear as to how the switch had been turned on. When they went to check, they saw only the cat scampering off with something it had found beneath the switchboard.

After the accident, Jibran lapsed into a deep depression bordering on paranoia. He became disoriented with his surroundings and suffered from amnesia, often misplacing personal belongings like money, keys, and worst of all – the chain with his mother's wedding ring.

Following medical advice, Veena took him to France. They stayed with close friends in Normandy in a late-medieval chateau. The presence of cats in the chateau disturbed Jibran greatly. He would not be pacified until they left the chateau and moved to a hotel.

Anything that reminded him of tragic events at home was likely to set him off. Even a passing resemblance of his psychoanalyst to Tariq, necessitated a change of therapist. He responded better to the substitute: a female psychiatrist, who reminded him of Bua.

Veena took Jibran for daily walks in the rural environment. She took care to avoid routes with wayside distractions like fountains or carved cisterns.

On a day trip to Biarritz, there was some concern when he insisted that the Madonna figure in a church painting resembled his mother. Recollection of his mother, prompted him to reach for the wedding ring for reassurance. He was distressed when he could not find it. Veena had to explain that he had probably left it at home.

❧

After several weeks of treatment, a moderately plump, calm Jibran travelled back to Karachi with Veena. He looked forward to the homecoming. Veena left him at the front door with Bua, promising to return later.

When Jibran entered his home, the cat bounded up and rubbed itself against his legs, purring contentedly. It followed him into the studio, jumping on to the divan.

'The poor wretch has been quite miserable without you,' Bua said. 'Even I felt sorry for it.'

Jibran smiled, reaching out to stroke it. The cat sat still.

As soon as Bua left, it began burrowing amongst the bolsters, searching for something it seemed to have secreted away – seizing it when spied and dropping it before Jibran like an offering. It was the chain strung with the wedding ring. In a flash, he recalled it catching on his cufflink and falling off when he approached the switchboard, that fateful evening.

In the dead of night, Jibran found himself in the garden. He was searching for *Pleiades,* a cluster of stars – six visible and one not – which encircled the mound in his mural. He panicked when he found no stars, no moon, but only the dark, dark sky. He decided to return to the studio, but stopped on seeing the wheelchair under the switchboard. As it began moving on its own up and down the veranda, tears streamed down his face. He turned away, stumbling instinctively towards the pool. Through the darkness – through the tears – he could discern the silvery sheen of leaping fish. But there was something else. Six pairs of shining eyes stared at him. The missing cats had returned.

In the morning, Bua found Jibran lifeless by the pool, eyes wide open. The cat sat beside him – purring.

Acknowledgements

At times, I look back with some surprise at the varied occupations of my working life. The moves between the different lines of work were usually prompted by chance or design. However, every opportunity was undertaken wholeheartedly, the interest being kept alive by the ticking of the meter in each enterprise.

The task of writing fiction is one such chance event. These stories may not have been written without the urging of Dr Adrian A. Husain who believed the exercise could be done and led me to it.

I am grateful to the inimitable Sadia Dehlavi for being the proverbial pillar; to Soraiya Qadir for reviewing some of the drafts. Her point of view combined deep affection with critical discernment. Kamil Rahim deserves special thanks for explaining the mechanics of computer operation to achieve certain results. Muneeza

Shamsi was a great help, as were her daughters, Kamila, Mashaal Gauhar, Zainab Omar and Saira Irshad, and also, Rohail Hyatt of Coke Studio.